JUST US

ff

JUST US

Gina Wilson

faber and faber

LONDON · BOSTON

First published in 1988
by Faber and Faber Limited
3 Queen Square London WC1N 3AU

Typeset by Boldface Typesetters, London EC1
Printed in Great Britain by
Richard Clay Ltd Bungay Suffolk

British Library Cataloguing in Publication Data

Wilson, Gina
Just us.
I. Title
823'.914[F]   PR6073.1465/
ISBN 0-571-15199-X

CHAPTER ONE

'Don't look so desperate!' said Lyn. Beth looked like someone taking aim at a dartboard, eyes narrowed, mouth screwed up to one side. 'You'd put anyone off. Smile or something!'

'What's there to smile about? There's only me and Sarah Jones never been asked out in the whole class.'

'Sarah couldn't care less.'

'She could. All that hockey and swimming's a big cover-up. Anyway, I don't care if she cares or not. *I* care.'

'You're not missing much. It's not all it's cracked up to be.'

'It is if you're really keen on each other.'

'So they say.'

Beth sighed. To Lyn's relief her face began to untwist and look reasonable again – thin and freckly, with a slight squint in one eye which an operation hadn't quite corrected. 'I worry at night, you know. I keep thinking I'll never get married.'

' There probably won't *be* marriages in a few years' time. I never give it a thought.'

Beth sighed again. 'It's different for you, though.'

Lyn left Beth's in time to be home for supper, but there was no one there. Clare had left a note on the kitchen table, saying she'd had to dash and there were beefburgers in the fridge. She'd obviously felt guilty because there was a row of kisses at the end. Lyn put it down. Just like old times! She supposed it was a good thing, really. Till recently, it had looked as if things would never get back to normal.

1

She picked up an apple and wandered into the sitting-room. A few months ago, Gran would still have been sitting there, pressed up to the window. 'Good God, Lynny! Who's this stoat? . . . . Oh, look! A trout! . . . Heaven help us! An *anteater*!' Lyn had frequently wondered what she thought she looked like herself – a parrot, maybe. Or, on days when she'd done herself up for visitors, a macaw. Today, she would have given a resigned sniff as Lyn walked in. 'She's out again, Lynny. Good job there's me, my dear, or you'd be properly left in the lurch.'

Lyn hunched on the edge of the settee, feeling hollow. Now, there wasn't Gran. They wouldn't be watching the telly later, Lyn with her feet up, Gran sipping 'medicinal' sherry and observing that they only had themselves to blame for spoiling Clare rotten. She wouldn't be sighing, for the millionth time, 'She could have taken the world by storm, Lynny. She gave it up for you. All for you.'

Ever since Lyn could remember, that had been Gran's constant lament. Early on, when she had been five or six, Lyn had believed it and felt miserable. But, one night, Clare had found her sobbing into her pillow and turned the light on again and told her it wasn't true. 'I wanted you more than anything,' she'd breathed, smelling of honey and gardenias. 'It's just Gran. She can't understand why I'm not famous. When you're a big girl she'll get big ideas for you too. It'll be your turn then.' But now Lyn was a big girl, and Gran was dead.

Clare came home at eleven twenty-five, precisely when Lyn was expecting her. The Bell closed at eleven ten and it took another fifteen minutes for Clare to make her farewells and wander down the road. Tonight, Lyn could hear her rummaging in her bag for keys, then trying one or two in the lock before hitting on the right one. She came in, pale and blowing on her hands, bringing all the smells of the pub with her. 'Have you been all right? I thought Beth might come round.'

2

'I spent the whole afternoon at Beth's.'

'I don't like the thought of you being on your own, though. I still hate it myself. It's so obvious then that she's not here.'

'I did a bit of French for next term.'

'*French* !' Clare squatted in front of the gas fire. 'Oh, you must have been feeling desperate.'

'I was OK.'

'*Abandoned*.'

'Don't keep going on. Either go out or stay in, but don't start agonizing.'

'Ah!' Clare stood up again and wandered towards the door, trailing the old fur coat that had belonged to her mother. 'I knew you were fed up. You're quite right to be. I've got a bit of news, actually. A gem. Never mind, it'll wait.'

Lyn let her go and leaned back, listening to her wandering along the passage to the kitchen. Her feet made the usual slurping noise on the lino. Funny, Lyn thought, how it was never anything obvious, like stumbling around, or slurring her speech, that gave the game away. It was the way the soles of Clare's feet never quite lost contact with the floor once she'd had a drink or two. However gracefully she managed the rest of herself, her feet became earthbound – the feet of someone very old. Actually, it had been hard to tell her apart from Gran sometimes, trailing down the hall at the dead of night.

She sat rather gloomily for another half-hour on her own, regretting her tetchiness. After all, it was the first time Clare had been out for months – since it happened, in fact. She'd spent all that time cooped up indoors, too stricken to see anyone.

Lyn gave herself a shake and turned off the fire. As she lined up the milk bottles on the front step, 'Nosy' Nigel from next door came out with his. 'How's your mum?' he whispered, leaning over the railings between them. 'She

3

was on cracking form down at the pub. Did she bring anyone home?' He craned forward, trying to see past Lyn into the hall.

'You're going to spike yourself, Mr King,' she said. 'I'll tell Mum you were asking.' She stepped back inside and banged the door. She could hear Nigel banging his and retreating into his own hall, just through the wall. He lusted after Clare – no other word for it, she thought – regardless of his cosy little-wife-and-two-kids. He was an arch-hypocrite. He went to Beth's church. Beth said he read the Bible in the service once or twice a month, looking over his specs at the congregation as if he'd made up the words himself. He had a university degree. Everyone knew that. But only a few people knew what his mind was really like. 'A sewer!' Beth sniggered when she said it. She was quoting her father. He had a university degree himself and knew what he was talking about.

In her bedroom, Lyn shivered. Days weren't so bad but, in the dark, a slimy chill seeped through the wall from the room next door. Four months ago, at first light, she'd found Gran there, grey and cold, under a little mound of blankets. The rooms were side by side on the ground floor, off the passage that led to the kitchen. Originally, they'd been one room but, towards the end, Clare had had a partitition wall erected so she and her mother could have adjoining bedrooms downstairs. Gran had kept a walking stick beside her bed to bang on the floor in emergencies but, eventually, she'd taken to banging all the time. That was when Lyn had offered to swop with Clare. 'At least take it in turns, Mum. Month and month about or something. She won't play me up half as much.' But it hadn't been easy, trying to decide when Gran was crying wolf and when she wasn't.

Lyn pulled her blankets up over her head. It would be pitch black in Gran's room, unless a sliver of moonlight was stealing in over the flat bed. It would be light on the stick still lying there, blanching it like an old thigh-bone. Gran

4

had banged it that last night. She had called. Lyn could still hear her calling . . . She turned over, drowning out the voice with creaks and the rustle of sheets. Clare had been urging her to sleep upstairs again. 'Stop tormenting yourself. It wasn't your fault.' But Lyn couldn't go. Not yet. It would be a second betrayal. In any case, next week new lodgers were arriving. Soon they'd be sneaking about at night, knocking into things and giggling. It would be all right then.

It was early September, just before the start of the new school year. The next day, Lyn caught a bus into the centre of Lamford and bought herself a new games skirt and gym shoes. On her way home, she stopped at Mrs Cardew's tiny terraced house in the next road to her own. She'd known Cardy all her life. Cardy and Gran had been best friends. 'She likes sharing you,' Gran had said. 'She's got no one of her own.' Cardy's husband had been dead for years – so long that when Lyn, as a little girl, had asked the colour of his eyes, Cardy had cast her own heavenward and exclaimed, 'Lord! What an odd question! However would I remember that?' Lyn had thought *that* was odd. But gradually she'd realized that Cardy didn't like looking back. Day by day, she bustled cheerfully on into the future. Her very appearance seemed to be cocking a snook at Time. Her hair was still coal-black and her compact little body spry as a sparrow's.

Today, she beamed broadly at Lyn. 'Just the person! Come in and hear my news.'

'What's up?' said Lyn. The hall smelled sharply of detergent. In the kitchen, purple and yellow freesias stood in a little glass vase in the middle of the table.

'Mrs Scott's been telling them down at The Bell about my spare room. There's a young man coming round at six to have a look. I might take him!'

5

'A lodger! You'd be upside-down in no time, Cardy. No hot water, no toilet-paper. He might bring girls in.'

Cardy shook her head. The young man Mrs Scott was sending had been brought up by a widowed mother. He wasn't a tearaway. 'He's a teacher, Lynny. Only just arrived in Lamford. This is his first post.'

'If he's only just escaped from his mother he'll probably start his "tearing away" right now. I can't see why you need anyone.'

'Your Gran's left a gap.' Cardy sighed. 'That's why. – Anyway, Clare likes her lodgers, doesn't she? I thought you'd approve.'

'She has those girls for the extra money. You always said our house was like a circus.'

'That's because Clare won't get organized.'

'Oh.' Lyn turned away. 'I can see you're soon going to be too busy for me!'

She spent the rest of the day at Beth's, bemoaning the fact that term was starting in three days' time but actually looking forward to it. Summer had been desolate. The sight of Clare, wan-faced and black-clad, had driven her, regularly, all but screaming, out into the streets. And there had been no relief at Cardy's, either. Beth's parents had welcomed her, day or night. They had encouraged her to move in with them indefinitely. 'Perhaps your mother needs to be on her own,' Mrs Hastings had suggested, 'coming to terms . . . and Mrs Cardew, too . . . ' At the beginning of August, they had invited her to go with them to Brittany. But she had stayed behind. She was sad herself; the Hastingses seemed to forget that. It had been her Gran, after all. Even Clare, now and again, had acknowledged that, and apologized for claiming sole right to their joint grief.

'Mum's a bit better these days,' she told Beth. 'She's actually started going down to The Bell again.'

'Leaving you on your own? Don't you mind?'

'Not really.'

6

Beth went on slowly brushing Lyn's long, straight hair. It hadn't been cut for five years and hung, fine and silky, to her waist. Her face was fine too, Beth thought – like a Japanese doll, smooth and oval, the eyebrows mere brush-strokes, the cheekbones high. Her eyes were different, of course. They were grey and open – you could tell what mood she was in, even if her thoughts were unfathomable. They were sitting in front of the mirror in Beth's bedroom. They had been listening to her tapes and brushing each other's hair into exotic styles. They had been laughing a lot. 'You look like an Afghan hound or something,' said Beth, trying to recapture the hilarity. 'Long hair's out. You should have yours cut like mine.'

'You look like a man,' said Lyn. 'You could walk into a Gents' anywhere and nobody'd spot the difference!' She screeched with laughter and Beth screeched too.

Later, as she cycled home in the dark, the screeching echoed in Lyn's head. Sometimes she and Beth laughed till the tears ran down their faces. That afternoon, the main joke had been Beth's fixation with boys. They'd agreed that she should only be allowed to 'go on' in five-minute bursts, and Lyn had actually timed her to make sure she didn't overrun. They'd had some of their screeches over that. But, really, it hadn't been funny at all. Beth was obviously working herself into a state, and, deep down, Lyn had found herself bored. You couldn't go on sympathizing for ever. Maybe she should *bribe* someone to take Beth out for a bit! Not Simon Reid, though . . .

Simon was in the year above Lyn at school. About six months ago, it had almost become serious between them – he had taken her to the pictures and kissed her there. He had kissed her in the kitchen at home too, and, once, in the sitting-room, when Gran had nodded off in front of the telly. But, at the very moment when Lyn had started to wonder if she could think of him as a 'steady', he had wrecked the whole thing. 'I like you easily the best, Nyl, but I've got a sort of thing about Sonia Cannelli's legs. It doesn't mean anything.' Unfortunately, Lyn had found it meant rather a lot to her. She'd refused to go out with him the next time he had asked her, and the time after. . . . Sonia Cannelli's legs had lasted a month – then it had been Christa Spenser's mouth, followed by Olivia Price's breasts. 'I still like you best. It's just . . . bits of other people.'

The centre of town was still alight. Lyn pedalled slowly, inspecting shop windows and jangling her bell at people she knew. Soon she'd be charging blindly through the dark side of town, trying to control her imagination. There was supposed to be a loony who ran about at night in Stavely Street without a stitch on. In Marlborough Road, women had been grabbed and dragged into a derelict yard . . .

By the time she approached Cardy's house, she was panting. The lights were all turned out. Cardy would be tucked up in her bed at the back. She'd be dreaming of her lodger. Perhaps he'd soon be installed in the big front bedroom, all cosy, with the curtains drawn against the night and just the glow of a lamp showing through.

Lyn reached home unscathed. She chained her bike to the railings outside, burst into the hall and leaned against the radiator, gasping for breath.

'Lyn!'

Lyn grinned. The old days! Clare was clad in a deeply-fringed green kimono that someone had brought back from China for Gran, about fifty years ago. 'What's going on? Who's here?'

'A VIP!' Clare's eyes flashed. 'Trapped in there! Just for you!'

Lyn allowed herself to be flapped, ahead of Clare, into the sitting-room. She expected to see one of Clare's pub cronies grinning up sheepishly from the sagging pouffe by the fire, someone familiar for whom Clare had decided to 'perform'. Instead, a complete stranger was perching on the front of

8

the sofa, staring into a brandy glass. He stood up and held out his hand.

'Sit down!' hooted Clare. 'No need to stand for Lyn, for Pete's sake!' She turned to Lyn. 'This is Matthew Beech – the bit of news I had for you last night, if you hadn't turned sour on me. I've just rescued him from The Bell. Mrs Scott was about to serve up one of her pasties. "Dog meat!" I said. "Come home with me and I'll feed you properly!" '

'Has she given you anything yet?' asked Lyn, uneasily. It was one thing for Clare to show off to friends . . .

Matthew Beech shook his head. He was fine, he said. The brandy was perfect.

'He's going to live at Cardy's, can you believe?' cried Clare. 'Kippers and mince every day!'

'I could heat up some soup.'

'Oh, sit down!' Clare pouted. 'You're spoiling everything – this sensitive flower of Academe is about to become your English teacher! That's the point! Sacrificing himself for the benefit of *Gledhill Comp*! Mad, isn't he? I've told him so!'

Lyn stood rooted to the middle of the floor as a deep flush burned its way slowly across her face.

'There! Knocked sideways!' crowed Clare. 'I told you she would be. The staff-room at Gledhill isn't exactly crammed with dishy young men.'

'*Mum*!' Lyn grabbed a nearby tray of dirty coffee things and backed out of the room, mumbling excuses. From the hall, she could hear the low rumble of Matthew Beech's voice, interrupted at intervals by swooping peals from Clare. How long had he been here? How long had Clare been in that idiotic state? The sitting-room door opened and Clare darted out. 'Why've you left us? It's so rude. He's absolutely charming.'

'You're plastered! You're making an exhibition of yourself!'

Clare's eyes flickered down to the tangled cord of her kimono. 'I'm not.' She blinked, and beamed defiantly. 'He says I'm the first spark of life he's seen in Lamford. He's thinking of joining The Players. As a matter of fact, I took him in my office and showed him all my things!'

CHAPTER TWO

Clare's 'office' was a tiny room just inside the front door.
Every house in the road had an identical cubby-hole, but
nobody was very sure of its original function. Nosy Nigel
had turned his into a tiled shower unit and the Fishers had
tucked the telephone away in theirs, along with their complete set of the *Encyclopaedia Britannica* and a tea-chest full of
back numbers of *National Geographic*.

At the Mellors', it was the corner where Gran had insisted
on storing all the relics of Clare's years in show-business.
Old press-cuttings, photographs, and faded programmes
lined the walls. On top of a small desk by the window was a
pile of fan mail dating back to the mid-sixties – 'the hectic,
madcap years,' Gran had sighed proudly, 'with stardom
but a curtain-call away!' People had thought she was being
funny, but she wasn't.

'God! Imagine taking him in there!' Beth kept saying in
Lyn's bedroom the following afternoon. 'Don't worry. He
probably thought she was fantastic. Really glamorous. At
least she's not boring like most mums.'

'He'll talk about it in the staff-room,' groaned Lyn. 'He'll
tell people like Mrs Ryder.'

'You know,' said Beth thoughtfully, 'she could be getting
menopausal, couldn't she? That makes some people go
weird.'

'Does it really!' The sight of Beth's freckly face, weighing
things up, infuriated Lyn suddenly. 'She's not geriatric, you

11

know. And she's not weird just because she doesn't spend her life sitting on church committees. As a matter of fact, I'm glad she's boozing again. She hadn't had much last night, you know. It's just she's been off it for months. She's not used to it.'

Later, on her own, she stretched out on the floor and listened to records. She'd been bitchy again. Beth had slunk off home with her tail between her legs. Whose fault was it? Was she really more irritating than ever these days, or was Lyn just finding her so for some reason? 'We could walk past Mrs Cardew's, Lynny, and have a little peer,' she had ventured, breaking a long silence. 'I'm dying to set eyes on him.'

'Well, I'm not. I want him to have a chance to forget me completely.'

Beth had eyed the wide black ribbon Lyn wore in a bow on top of her head. 'No chance of that! Nobody ever does forget you. You're one of those people who makes an impression. Dad says you're disturbing . . . '

Lyn sighed and flicked over the pages of a magazine that Beth had brought. They'd patch it up at school. People were always rowing with their best friends, it didn't mean anything.

Mr Beech was introduced to the whole school at the opening assembly of term. The Head asked him to stand up so everyone could see who he was.

'Poor thing!' whispered Beth, ' – us all gaping at him! He looks OK, I don't think you need to be scared.'

'I'm not. "Embarrassed" was what I said.'

The day had started badly. Beth had been waiting for her in the cloakroom, blinking back tears. 'I've been put down to Div Two in English,' she'd whispered. 'That was the only thing I thought I was any good at. Mum and Dad'll be all depressed. And now you and I don't have *any* classes the same. We'll never see each other.'

'They can't put you down now. We're half-way through the course. It's mad!'

'Mrs Ryder's just been along to see me – specially. She says as there's a massive upheaval anyway, with Mr Stacey leaving, it won't make any difference. She says Mr Stacey said I'd be more "*comfortable*" in Div Two.' The tears began to spill.

'Who're we having, anyway? Her?'

'Mr Beech. Both divs.'

'*God*!'

'Well, he's Mr Stacey's replacement.'

Lyn watched Mr Beech's profile now as he sat down at the side of the hall and ran a hand through his black hair. For a second, she glimpsed a high, white brow underneath – fragile – then the hair flopped back again. Beth was right. Awful to be gawped at. He'd hated it. She felt relieved; he wouldn't be the sort to yammer on about coming to her house, then. There wouldn't be jokes about Clare.

At break, Beth was still bleak. 'How are we ever going to see each other?'

'There's now. And lunch-time.'

'You don't care, do you?'

'I do. But it's only five periods a week. It doesn't make that much difference.'

'Five periods when I felt equal to you for once.' Beth turned and wandered away.

Lyn watched her go, hunched and hangdog. It was Beth's parents who caused all the misery. Div Two for everything didn't actually mean you were thick, but they thought it did. Not that they said so in as many words, but their faces froze in a certain expression. Lyn had seen it often enough. And she'd seen the reverse of it too, when, however ruefully, they had praised her to the skies for her own successes at school.

'Wotcha, Nyl!' Simon Reid clapped her on the shoulder. He'd obviously spent the summer abroad. The whites of his blue eyes stood out against his deeply tanned skin, making him look oddly surprised all the time. 'What's ailing Beth the Death?'

'Nothing. Don't be so rude. Well done in the exams, by the way. Did you really get five As?' He grinned. His teeth were shiny white too. 'Where did you get that tan? *Very* smooth!'

'Spain.'

'I didn't go anywhere. Gran died, you know.'

He hadn't known. Under the tan he went red. He gestured awkwardly. 'I'm really sorry, Nyl.'

'Mum took it badly.'

'God . . .'

'She's pulling round. She's started going down to the pub again, bringing people home. She actually brought that new Mr Beech back a couple of days ago!' Blast! She hadn't meant to spread that round. It was just that Simon had looked so flummoxed, not knowing how to react to Gran . . .

'Oh, him! He's quite a guy! Took us first period. He's editor-in-chief of the school magazine. I got myself elected on to the committee. If you want something in, I can fix it!'

'If I want something in, it'll get in on merit!'

'He wants really decent poetry, he says.'

'Where does he think he's going to get it from?'

'I said there was a girl in Upper Five H whose initials were L.M. who . . .'

'You didn't!'

Simon reached out and plucked at her bow. 'No, I didn't, as it happens!' He loped off, leaving her to tie her hair up again.

The last lesson before lunch was English. Mr Beech came in with a pile of Shakespeares and sent someone off to the bookroom for the rest. He looked agitated, running his eyes back and forth over the twenty-odd faces in front of him as if someone had given him five minutes to memorize the lot.

14

He asked twice if the class had read *The Tempest* already. 'Mrs Ryder wanted me to make quite sure Mr Stacey hadn't started on it last year,' he muttered as they assured him they'd never seen it before. The books were distributed and most of the lesson was spent reading aloud. Lyn was not chosen for a part and sat at the back, with her head well down, until five minutes before the bell. Then, for no reason that she could think of afterwards, she looked up, straight into Mr Beech's eyes. After that, she couldn't follow the words properly. Her heart raced. He'd been staring at her, remembering her tipsy mother with the roomful of junk, deciding she was a no-hoper with a background like that.

The bell went and she scooped her things into her bag and slipped out into the corridor behind a knot of others. He was there, dithering about which direction to take, and asking the way to the staff dining-room. 'We must see that you get a part next time, Lyn. Have you inherited your mother's dramatic talent?'

'Not in the least.' Lyn hugged her bag to her chest and kept going. 'I'm not like her at all.'

Beth had saved her a place in the canteen queue. 'I've got English after this. I was really looking forward to watching the look on Mr Beech's face when he caught sight of you, sitting there.'

'I've just had him,' said Lyn. 'You've missed nothing. He didn't know who I was.'

'No kidding! What a wet!'

But, by the end of the afternoon, Beth had changed her tune. 'Wow! He's *fabulous*! Why didn't you say? We're doing D. H. Lawrence. He stood there, never turning a hair, talking about all the symbolism and *sex* and everything! It was brilliant! Nobody sniggered or made any cracks, not even Kevin Williams, and you know what he's like.' She invited herself to the Mellors' for tea. 'We might

15

bump into him, Lyn, in Wellington Place. He might talk to us. God, one of these nights, he'll probably come round to your house again, if he likes Clare.'

'He doesn't.'

Outside Mrs Cardew's, an old white Mini was pulling up. Beth gripped Lyn's arm. '*Him*!' She scurried ahead. 'Mr Beech! Mr Beech!' Lyn watched him turn, his arms full of folders and text-books. 'I was in one of your classes this afternoon. I was near the back. We all thought it was great. I'm going to start on *Sons and Lovers* tonight.'

'Good.'

'I'm just going round to Lyn's.' Lyn was reaching them now. Mr Beech nodded at her. 'She lives round the corner.'

'I know. The Mellors gave me a marvellous welcome the other night.'

'Cardy's looking out of her window,' murmured Lyn. 'I think we're holding you up.'

Beth found herself propelled away along the pavement. 'Why did you have to say that? He didn't mind talking to us. – He obviously enjoyed himself at your place. You didn't need to fuss.'

'He couldn't say much else.'

'It's his eyes – don't you think so? They look as if they can see right through you.'

'Can't say I've noticed.'

It was midnight on Friday and Lyn was in bed. The new lodgers had arrived, as expected, and already she had adjusted to the bathroom being permanently occupied and the phone ringing non-stop. Actually, the girls weren't bad. One of them had arrived with fourteen pairs of shoes and told Lyn she could borrow any that fitted. They were both eighteen and had signed on for a term's cookery course at the Poly. Twice, already, they had brought home special soups to share with Lyn and Clare and the next week they were going on to puddings, they said.

This evening, Clare had taken them down to The Bell to introduce them to The Players – members of The Lamford Players, an amateur dramatic society of which she was the leading light. The Players met regularly in the gloomy little back bar – Mrs Scott booked it for them every Friday night – but, on almost any night of the week, one or two of them would be there somewhere. Gran had been right, Lyn thought, when she had remarked that they were 'nothing but a bunch of soaks'. It was years since they had staged a production of any size. Nosy Nigel was about the only member who didn't go for the beer – and he went to ogle Clare, which was worse. Someone had made the mistake of inviting him along after hearing him read in church. Fantastic voice production, they'd said. *Huh* !

Lyn wasn't expecting anybody home yet. Usually one of the Players invited the rest back to coffee at closing time. In the very old days, Clare had sometimes brought a gang back to Barnton Road. Gran had always stayed up late for that, hoping to kindle a spark of ambition, but people had just nodded and smiled amiably at her and lapsed into rambling anecdotes. Sometimes Clare had been persuaded to don an old costume and do a turn. That had been long, long ago – Lyn could remember herself, tucked in a corner in her dressing-gown, watching everyone watching Clare, joining in the clapping at the end. Gran's eyes had glistened. '*Now* tell me she couldn't have been a star!'

At the very moment when she got out of bed to turn off her light, Lyn heard the creak of the front door and the clumsy tip-toe of people trying not to be heard. She stood in the dark as they passed by on the other side of her door, heading for the kitchen. Someone sneezed. 'Shh,' hissed Clare. 'He's Lynny's teacher, for Pete's sake! He's got his reputation to think of!' There were stifled snorts and then the kitchen door closed.

Lyn crept back to bed and lay on her back, straining for

17

murmurings and sounds of merriment. Matthew Beech had come again. He was there, in the kitchen, with Clare and the students and anyone else who'd tagged along. Clare had probably got out the pink cigarettes Gran had ordered for her from Harrod's last Christmas. She would be making everyone laugh – and he'd be watching.

CHAPTER THREE

'I'm pretending I don't know he was there,' Lyn told Beth. 'It's nothing to do with me. He obviously doesn't think Mum's a drunken old bag, anyway. That was all I was worried about.'

'Course she's not an old bag. He probably fancies her.'

'Don't be stupid. She's twice his age.'

There was a silence. 'Anyway,' said Beth, 'you'll be interested to know he's just given me a C for a *Sons and Lovers* essay – and Dad did most of it, so it should have been good. D'you think he's a stiff marker? What did you get?'

'He doesn't give us the same topics.'

'What did you get for whatever your last topic was?'

'An A minus.'

Beth groaned. 'God! – D'you think maybe he's giving you high marks just to keep in with Clare?'

'I don't usually tell her what I get.'

'He doesn't know that.' Beth's face was turning sly. It often did these days, Lyn thought – ever since Ryder had moved her down a div. 'She's a bit of a flirt, you know, Lyn.'

'Who?'

'Clare. One of Dad's friends goes in The Bell a bit. He's not exactly flattering about her.'

'That's probably because he fancies her himself and she's not interested. Like Nigel King. He has a dig at her every now and again, and the whole world knows he'd give his eye-teeth to have it off with her.'

Beth gave a little snigger. 'That's gross! You can't talk like that about your own mother! My parents worry about you, you know. They don't think it's right, the way you're being brought up.'

'My God! And what they do to you is "right", is it?'

'They don't do anything to me.'

'All the endless nagging at you to be brilliant.'

Beth twitched. 'At least Mum keeps our house clean. There aren't heaps of dirty clothes on the landing, and mouldy food in carrier bags all over the place.'

The shrill taunt hung in the air for a few seconds. 'If you find us that disgusting,' Lyn remarked quietly, 'you don't need to come round again.'

At that, Beth crumpled against the cloakroom wall and burst into tears. 'I don't mean it. You know I like Clare. I'm sorry. Mum and Dad are so boring. I'm boring. Mr Beech must think so or he wouldn't give me such dreggy marks.'

'Who cares?' said Lyn. 'Since when was he the be-all and end-all?'

'Since day one.' Beth's head dropped on her chest. 'Don't tell me you haven't noticed. I'm completely batty about him.'

In the end, she allowed Lyn to help her into her coat and they left school together. At the Mellors', Clare took one look at them and produced a *bombe surprise* from the freezer. 'Lorna made this yesterday. She got an A for it in "Cream Desserts". Heaven knows what we'd pay if we were out!' They sat, all three, round the table with glass bowls and tea-spoons. The ice-cream was rich and very sweet. 'Lorna feels sick at the sight of it,' said Clare. 'That's the trouble when you make things. You can't be bothered to eat them yourself.' Lyn and Beth smiled weakly. 'Have you two been at each other's throats again?'

'We're all right,' muttered Lyn.

'We like each other, really,' Beth said. 'We just seem to get on each other's nerves sometimes – that's the trouble.'

20

She stayed the night, curled up on the camp-bed in Lyn's room in an old sleeping-bag which she left there permanently for that purpose. 'Promise you'll do your homework properly,' whispered Mrs Hastings down the phone. 'Get Lyn to test you if it's learning.' But, instead, they talked all evening and half the night about everything other than school work. At least, Beth talked. Lyn didn't mind. She didn't want to get going herself. You could say a lot of daft things in the middle of the night and feel a fool in the morning. Besides, for once, Beth was being quite interesting, analysing her crush on Mr Beech. She knew of at least two or three other girls who were mad on him too, she said. They thought he was sensitive. He took them seriously. 'It's his *eyes*!' Beth hugged herself. ' . . . Don't you find that?'

Later on, Lyn couldn't sleep. She lay in the dark, hands behind her head, knees crooked, listening to Beth's settled breathing. When she'd talked herself out, Beth had yawned contentedly. 'I'm a great blabbermouth, aren't I? God, I feel better, though! You should have talked too, Lynny.'

'I'm a listener.'

'Rubbish. You just bottle things up. You should let it all spill out. That's what friends are for.'

Lyn turned over and closed her eyes. Either friends weren't for that or she'd never had any. Down near the floor, Beth whimpered and stirred. Lyn smiled. Beth *was* a friend – someone to count on. That was it! They counted on each other.

'Beth's worked herself into quite a state over Mr Beech.'

Clare turned from the sink. At the kitchen table, Lyn was bent over Maths prep. 'What sort of state?'

'A crush, I suppose. When he gives her rotten marks she goes into a big depression.'

'Perhaps she's just not much good at English.'

Lyn looked up. 'Could you say something to him, in the pub?'

' I can't tell him his job.'

'You do see him, though, don't you?'

'Now and again.' Clare had slipped quietly back into her old habit of dropping in at The Bell for an hour or two most evenings. She might as well, she'd said. Lyn had her homework to do, and the lodgers were usually around if she finished early and wanted company.

'How many times has he been back here?'

'Two or three. You must be able to hear when I've got people in. There's nothing to stop you joining us, you know.'

'He's my teacher.'

'Not when he's here, he's not.'

It was well and truly autumn, with wet gusty days, and nights drawing in. The Head gave frequent warnings in Assembly of the dangers of slippery leaves. People on detention were sent out to the main quad with shovels and black plastic sacks to clear them up.

One evening, Lyn left school late. Miss Turner had kept half the chemistry class behind for fooling in the lab. Nobody had confessed to nudging Cheryl Bates when she was trying to do something delicate with a test-tube and tongs, so Miss Turner had decided to blame everyone on the bench. It didn't matter, Lyn thought. It had been worth it to see Cheryl mopping up a mess for once. She wandered along, scuffing leaves with her feet and staring up at the sky. Mr Beech wanted an atmospherical poem about autumn for the school magazine. He'd offered a five pound prize for the best . . . You could have the sunset sky as a battle-field, Lyn thought – all bruised and blood-streaked. You could have the clouds, like dappled chargers, thundering across, and the black branches of trees reaching up out of the mud,

22

like the flailing arms of the dying. She groaned to herself. You could have no such thing! She turned the corner into Wellington Place. It was pitch dark the minute you came down out of the sky! '*Ah*!'

Someone had stepped, out of nowhere, right into her path.

'Lyn!' It was Mr Beech. 'Sorry.' He bent down and picked up her bag. He held her elbow. 'I've frightened the life out of you.'

'It's OK.' Lyn's knees were knocking. Her heart was pounding. She could make his face out quite easily now. 'I was trying to think of a poem – for autumn, you know.'

'I've probably wrecked it.'

'It wasn't much good anyway.'

'Seriously,' he said, 'I've been looking for the chance to have a quiet word. You're doing some excellent work for me this term. You know that, don't you?'

'Thank you.'

'I just wondered how far ahead you'd planned. Have you settled on your A-levels yet?'

'Well, English, I hope. Probably French. The third one's a bit uncertain.'

He nodded. 'Some of the others have discussed it with me already, that's all. If I have a criticism of you, Lyn, it's that you're not quite forthcoming enough – for your own good.' He patted her on the shoulder and took a step away in the direction of his car, parked at the kerb-side. 'Let me know if I can help.'

Lyn turned to go.

'Remember what I said.'

Which bit of what he'd said? She was still shaking. 'Yes. Thank you very much.'

He carried on watching her intently through the gloom, but his hand was on the car door now. He'd finished with her really. She started to walk away. 'You were right. You don't take after your mother, do you?' she thought he said.

At tea, she stared silently at Clare – at the never-still

23

mouth, the flickering, self-doubting eyes. She was woeful, really; that's what she was – behind all the fun and laughter.

'What's on your mind?' said Clare, laying down her knife and fork.

'Would you say we were alike?'

'You're like your father.' Clare sighed.

The students raised inquiring eyes, wondering if she was going to say more. But she didn't. At her end of the table, Lyn carried on eating. She could feel his hand again on her elbow – holding her. He had been very close.

From then on, every time she approached Cardy's, she felt a quickening inside. Was he about to jump out again, and take her arm, and say more nice things? One evening, there was a sharp rap on the front window. She shot round, but it was only Cardy herself, shading her eyes to see out into the dark, and beckoning. She drew Lyn inside and led her along to the kitchen. 'You haven't been to see me for ages.'

'I thought you'd be up to your eyes with Mr Beech. How's it going?'

'Fine.' Cardy ran water into her kettle and plugged it in. She took biscuits, one by one, from a tin and arranged them on a willow-pattern plate. 'As a matter of fact I wanted to talk to you about him.'

'*Me*?' Lyn felt herself going red. God! Any minute Cardy would turn round and start jumping to conclusions.

But Cardy was fiddling with the teapot, spooning tea into it from her Coronation caddy. 'I just wondered . . . ' she spoke in a rush ' . . . if there was anything in the gossip I've been hearing – about him losing his head over Clare.'

'Oh!'

'It's none of my business – except in a way, of course, it is – with him being new here and Clare being the way she is . . . '

'She's just friendly. It doesn't mean a thing.'

'Exactly.'

'People are eaten with jealousy because she's so popular. They love making out she's an old slag.'

'I never said that, Lyn. Nothing like it.'

'He probably does like her. I expect he thinks she's fun. She *is*. I don't see why she shouldn't be, after all the misery . . . I'm really glad she's getting back to normal. So what if she goes over the top now and again? Gran always used to make allowances.'

'I should think she did – as it was all her fault in the first place.' Cardy sat down and patted Lyn's hand. 'Don't let's fight. You know I'm fond of Clare. She exasperates me, that's all. When's she ever going to grow up? Never, I suppose. I ought to stop waiting for the day.'

They sat, facing each other, avoiding each other's eyes. They'd had conversations like this before. Basically, Cardy regarded Clare as a flibbertigibbet. She didn't altogether blame her for it. Given her upbringing, she could hardly have been anything else. All her mother's doing, of course. Cardy helped herself to a biscuit. Maybe, if she were to be honest, she would hold herself ever so slightly responsible too. Someone ought to have stood up to Annie Utting . . .

Cardy could remember the day Clare was born, pretty from the start, in an elfin way. Annie couldn't wait to get her on the stage. It was in the family, she said, and anyone could see the child was beautiful. Vincent Utting had hated the idea but Annie had steam-rollered on, arranging ballet lessons and tap-dancing, riding, elocution, music. In the end, poor Vincent had actually died the very week of Clare's drama school auditions! Annie had always held that to account for her lack of success. How could you possibly look your best with a death in the family? How could you launch yourself into comic parts?

She had sent Clare away to an obscure little college in France to recover from her disappointment, and there, at the age of nineteen, she had married an English youth who had come to study cuisine and hotel-management in the same town. Annie had been devastated. And yet it had been entirely thanks to Geoffrey that a tiny taste of success had eventually come Clare's way. Back in England, he had opened a small bistro beside a theatre in the heart of Manchester, and his show-business clientèle had developed a soft spot for Clare. For three or four years, they had put a succession of minor roles her way – until she had become pregnant with Lyn.

The pregnancy had come as the second severe blow to Annie. 'Come down here,' she'd begged. 'I can look after the baby. London's no distance. You'll get loads of work with your experience.'

Geoffrey had been stonily opposed to the idea, but Annie had won. Clare had moved back, bringing Lyn with her. She had no choice, she said – her mother had sacrificed everything for her. A few months later, Geoffrey had sold up and followed them. He had bought a honeysuckle cottage a few miles from Lamford and they had set up home together again. But the sweetness had gone. Geoffrey felt betrayed. Clare's mother had come first, and always would. It was only his attachment to Lyn that kept the marriage going for another eighteen months.

' . . . I'm over-protective of Matthew,' said Cardy at last. 'I know I am. He wouldn't thank me for it. I suppose it's because it's such a long time since I had anyone to look after.'

'What about me?'

Cardy squeezed her hand. 'Of course, there's you, Lynny. Always will be. Annie used to say I understood you better than her and Clare put together! Did you know that? At one time, there was quite a grain of truth in it . . . But it's different now she's gone. Has to be. You and Clare must stick together now. I wouldn't want to intrude on that.'

'Cardy's getting very hot and bothered about Matthew

Beech,' Lyn announced after supper. 'Someone's been giving her ideas.'

'Have they?' Clare raised her eyebrows. She had been examining them in a hand-mirror, tweaking them into shape with a pair of sharp tweezers.

'She doesn't want him falling for your charms.'

'What charms? I'm old enough to be his mother.'

'You don't look it,' said one of the lodgers obligingly.

'Don't I, really?'

That night, Matthew Beech came home from the pub again with Clare. From an upstairs window, Lyn caught sight of them striding down the street, hands in their pockets, faces turned towards each other. Clare was wearing the tatty fur-coat, with a red shawl draped over her head. As Lyn watched, the wind whisked the end of the shawl high into the air. Matthew caught it. They stopped right outside Nosy Nigel's while he tucked it back inside her collar. Then, for a second or two, they just stood, looking at each other. Lyn was startled. They're going to kiss! she thought. But they didn't, and she ran downstairs to be in the kitchen when they came in.

'I've a feeling Cardy wouldn't like you being here, Mr Beech,' she remarked as he settled himself at the table.

'She can call you Matthew, can't she?' said Clare, ' . . . in our own kitchen.'

'Course she can.'

He didn't ask her about Cardy. Maybe he hadn't heard, Lyn thought. He was looking young. The wind had whipped colour into his face. But it had drained Clare. Beside him, she looked cold and rather wrinkly.

CHAPTER FOUR

'You must tell us how you're faring with the wonderful Mr Beech, Lyn,' said Mrs Hastings, placing her elbows on the very edge of the dining-table and clasping her hands under her chin.

Lyn enjoyed this stage of dinner at the Hastingses' – when the plates had been cleared away and they sat on, talking, by candle-light, and drinking. She and Beth were allowed wine too, in special long-stemmed glasses. At home, Clare and the students would be having soggy lasagne and maybe some lettuce sprinkled with bottled French dressing. The Laura Ashley oil-cloth would still have sticky patches from breakfast. Here, she and Beth faced each other across an expanse of starched linen. Lyn wiped her mouth on a napkin. Clare would grimace and say it was all too *genteel* for words, but, actually, Lyn didn't mind. Doing things the Hastings way was a challenge to her adaptability, she'd decided (as doing things the Mellor way must be to Beth's). Anyway, the Hastingses had a way of flattering her. They valued her opinions. They made her realize she *had* opinions.

'Mr Beech? Fine.'

'Beth says he's become something of a family friend.'

'He goes to the same pub as Mum and comes back for coffee sometimes.'

'And then you have to be on your best behaviour, I expect!'

'I'm often in bed by the time they get back.'

'I wouldn't be,' said Beth. 'I'd stay up specially.'

'Beth has become besotted,' grunted Mr Hastings. 'We get Mr Beech morning, noon and night!'

'He's having that effect on quite a few people,' said Lyn. She liked Mr Hastings. He was rich, but ordinary – always saying how 'bloody hard' he'd worked.

'Not you, though.'

'No.' Lyn noted his slightly narrowed eyes. He's peeved, she thought. If Beth's gone daft, he wants everyone else to be too.

'Why not?' said Mr Hastings. 'Why are you such a cool customer?'

'Lyn's always different,' said Beth ruefully. 'Aren't you, Lyn?'

Lyn shook her head. Mr Hastings was still watching her but his face was relaxing now, more curious than hostile. 'I remember what Lyn likes.' He lit a panatella from one of the candles and blew a thin stream of smoke in her direction. 'You like the smell of cigars, don't you? I remember that from last time.'

'Lyn likes all the best things,' murmured Mrs Hastings agreeably. She was smiling, dry dimples pitting her cheeks. 'How's your mother, dear? Is she getting over her bereavement now? Does she still miss your Gran terribly?'

'We both do.'

'They were so close, though, weren't they? It's awfully sad. Do you think you and your mum are going to be the same? It must be nice, in some ways, just the two of you. Are you great friends?'

At the ends of her shoes, Lyn could feel her toes curling into claws. How could you answer a question like that? What the hell did it mean – *really* . . . ? Mr Hastings was blowing smoke rings, his face turned to the ceiling, but his ears straining for her reply. 'The same as you and Beth, I suppose.'

It was a Friday, and Lyn was staying the night. 'Funny,

29

how we sit round the table, all pally,' she said to Beth at bed-time, 'and yet you say they're really critical the minute my back's turned – about Mum and everything.'

'It's only because she's unusual,' said Beth cautiously. 'I mean, they're so conventional themselves, she probably frightens them.' She gave a little titter. 'I mean, she can be quite alarming . . . When I first met you, I never knew how she was going to be. Always friendly, but . . . you know . . . what she'd be wearing and if any of her friends would be there . . . Anyway, Mum and Dad think you and I are good for each other. Heaven knows why!'

In fact, she had often overheard her parents discussing Lyn. Despite their reservations about arrangements at Barnton Road, they admired her – her success at school, her resilience and pluck. They hoped some of these qualities might rub off on Beth and, in return, they felt Lyn was bound to benefit from experiencing their more 'traditional' life-style.

'It'll be bedlam at home,' Lyn whispered. She pulled the crisp sheets up under her chin. 'The girls finished some exams today. They're having a rave-up tonight.'

'Mr Beech might be there,' said Beth. 'Clare's probably asked him. You know, if I really concentrate, I can see his eyes in the dark!'

'No wonder your dad's worried!'

'He could be sitting in your kitchen, this very minute!'

'With all the booze and smoke. Someone usually starts frying bacon and eggs at about one in the morning. There's a disgusting fug.'

'Artistic people are like that. They're into ideas. They don't see the mess.'

Lyn rolled up into a ball. 'Nobody in our house has ideas!'

She left at noon the next day. No one would be up yet, at home. The curtains would all be drawn, like the week Gran died. It would be stale and dark inside. Outside, there was a damp chill in the air. In Wellington Place, children were jumping up and down under the towering horse-chestnut. Conkers are boring! Lyn thought, feeling old. Beyond the tree, she could see Cardy, out on the pavement in front of her house, peering up and down like a mole.

'Matthew didn't come in all night, Lyn. His bed hasn't been slept in.'

'Didn't he phone?'

'Not a squeak.'

'The girls do that, sometimes. Mum's always mad because she doesn't know if they've been murdered or raped. They never have, of course . . . ' She linked arms with Cardy and they went indoors. 'He'll be fine. Men can look after themselves. He's just been a bit thoughtless. It won't have crossed his mind you're going to worry.'

Cardy pulled back a little, her head on one side. 'And you wouldn't have the remotest idea where he is, I don't suppose . . . '

'How on earth would *I* know? I've been staying at Beth's.'

'Oh, I see. You're not going to tell me, you mean.' Cardy's mouth snapped shut.

Lyn escaped. The children were still squealing under the big tree but she didn't hear them. How could Cardy turn cold with her like that – and suspicious – after all the years they'd been close? Cardy's was the first name she'd learned to say. It was Cardy who had taken her to feed the ducks on Wotton Pond whenever Gran was bored with babysitting and Clare was in London, hiring herself out for tooth-paste ads. Cardy had taught her to read. But now she was cold. All because of Matthew bloody Beech! She thought he had spent a night of debauchery at Barnton Road with Clare and her cronies. She thought he was still there. She thought Lyn knew all about it . . .

Lyn pushed the front door open gingerly. The familiar, dank smell was pervading the hall. 'Squalid!' Gran had called it. It had given her grim pleasure to clear everything up before anyone was awake and then sit looking martyred all day. No one was stirring. Lyn paused outside the sitting-room door. He might be in there. If he was, it would probably be better not to know. She should go straight to the kitchen and start clattering round, giving him the chance to sneak away . . .

The door creaked as she pushed it open, but the figure on the sofa didn't move. Lyn crossed the room on tip-toe and drew back the curtains. 'Time to get up,' she said, without turning round. 'Now it's autumn, you ought to drive into the country round here and look at the trees.'

There was an upheaval behind her and, when she did turn round, Matthew Beech was sitting bolt upright, buttoning the collar of his shirt. 'Must have dropped off,' he muttered. His cheeks looked very pale above his dark chin. At the back, his hair stuck out in spiky tufts.

'Cardy's having a nervous breakdown in the street. You didn't tell her you were staying out. I'm sure she's guessed you're here. She'll hold it against Mum, you know. She thinks she's leading you astray.'

'She should mind her own business.'

'You are her business – she thinks so, anyway.' Lyn opened the window. 'I'd get out of this fug if I were you.' She didn't look at him again. He was probably hating her, thinking none of it was her business either.

In the kitchen, she turned on the radio and began clearing the table. 'Lyn!' It was him, in the doorway behind her. She didn't look. 'Can I help?'

'It's OK. Cardy'll still be worrying.'

'Why don't you come with me this afternoon – in the car? You can tell me where to go.'

She nodded. That was all – nothing spoken. By the time she thought of asking when, and if he meant Clare too, he'd gone. She filled the dish-washer and wiped down the table in a daze. No, she wouldn't waken Clare. If Clare came, the students would probably decide to come too, and, before she knew where she was, she'd be the only one that couldn't be fitted into the car. Besides, he hadn't actually mentioned any of the rest of them.

At two o'clock, there was a quick toot outside. Lyn had been sitting in Gran's chair. She'd already seen the Mini, nosing along the narrow road, and leapt to her feet.

'No sign of the others yet?' he said as she climbed in. 'Still dead to the world?'

'D'you want me to get them? I wasn't sure who you wanted exactly.'

'You'll do!' She glanced at him quickly, but he was staring anxiously through the windscreen at banks of dark cloud massing overhead.

At this stage, Lyn was still thinking that, whatever happened, Beth would be agog when she heard about it next day. 'God!' she'd howl. 'Why do *you* have all the luck? It's not fair!' But, by night-time, she had resolved to tell Beth nothing. She'd be eaten with jealousy and insist on getting the wrong idea. In any case, what was the *right* idea? Lyn herself hadn't been able to sort that out yet. She never would if Beth started distorting everything.

'Let's not look at trees,' he'd said after a mile or two, as rain spattered heavily on the windscreen. 'Let's talk. I want to get to know you, Lyn Mellor.'

Goose-flesh had prickled up the back of Lyn's neck. Teachers *never* wanted to know you. 'There's nothing to know. Well, I suppose there's a bit.'

He pulled into a lay-by and switched off the engine. Rain streamed down the windscreen and drummed on the roof. 'We'll start with the bit, then.' He smiled.

He didn't smile often, she thought. That was probably why it felt as if something extraordinary was happening. The smile faded, but he carried on looking at her. His eyes were so deep-set that you could imagine that he was viewing you from the very depths of himself.

'It's a bit unnerving, you know, the way you look at people.'

33

He turned away. 'That's a nerve! Yours is the blankest stare I've ever faced in my life! In class, I never know what's in your mind, or what you're about to come out with.'

'Do I really stare?'

'You'll be staring now, only I'm not allowed to look! You'll be watching me, with those solemn, round eyes. You'll be trying to work out what to tell your mother and Beth Hastings!'

'I shan't tell them anything.'

'I hope you're going to tell *me* a few things.' He faced her again. 'For instance, do you mind my coming round to your house? Does it bother you that I'm friendly with Clare? You were right, Mrs Cardew's absolutely opposed . . . She says, for one thing, it makes difficulties for you. Is that true? Do you mind?'

'Not now. I did at first, because I thought you might think Mum was rather mad and go talking about her at school.'

'Mrs Cardew seems to think I'm a bit infatuated. Did she tell you that?'

'I said it was rubbish.'

'Clare fascinates me. I find her riveting at times. She keeps that lot at the pub going, doesn't she? They adore her.'

'They keep her going too. She needs to be adored – not by anybody in particular. Just an audience.'

'Did you work that out yourself?'

'It's what Gran used to say.'

'And what did she say about you? Do you need to be adored too?'

'I don't know.' Lyn blushed crimson. There was nothing she could do about it. She gave an awkward little laugh. Out of the blue, it struck her that they were going to kiss one another. It was just going to happen . . . Maybe he'd thought of it first. Maybe it was all his idea. She felt boiling hot suddenly but sat absolutely still, zipped up in her jacket.

'What are you thinking about?'

34

'Cardy – the way she fusses. As if you were a little boy.'

'She means well.'

'When I was little, she used to look after me. They sort of shared me out – Mum, Gran and Cardy. Sometimes I slept in that room you've got now, in that very bed.'

'She's told me about it. You must have wondered where you really belonged.'

'The only time I wondered that was when I went out to the States to see Dad. He's married to someone else, you know. They've got two little kids now. I knew I didn't belong there.'

'Poor Lynny,' he murmured, and the goose-flesh prickled again.

Outside, the beat of the rain turned gradually to a patter. The sky was streaked grey and deep purple. 'Come on,' he said. 'You belong with me. Let's walk. People won't know what to think if we tell them we've sat in the car all afternoon!'

What *should* they think? Lyn wanted to ask as she picked her way along the road beside him, shivering and side-stepping round puddles. *Would* she have kissed him if it had come to it? Maybe something about him would have put her off – the unfamiliar smell of him, or the feel of his skin. Would she want to be squeezed right up to him, mouth to mouth? Where had the idea come from in the first place?

At home, Clare was stretched out on the settee with a cold cloth over her forehead. She thanked Lyn, rather distantly, for the note she'd left. 'Where did you get to?'

Matthew had come in too. Lyn brought them both a cup of tea and went off to her bedroom. She wanted to look at herself in the mirror – to see the 'round, solemn eyes' as *he* saw them. And her lips – how would he describe those? And all the rest of her?

As it got dark, she lay on her bed with her eyes shut, hearing his voice again, feeling his touch. She missed tea. Somewhere else in the house, people were moving

35

around and talking. He was still here, but he was with *them* now . . .

'You and I will have to have a talk.' The light had snapped on and Clare was there. She must have been having a bath; she was wearing a dressing-gown and had a towel wrapped round her head.

'What time is it?'

'Nine. Have you been asleep or what? Why did you vamoose as soon as you came in? Matthew wondered what he'd done.'

'He should have known.'

'Known?'

'That he hadn't done anything.'

'Oh.' Clare sat down on the end of the bed, untied the towel and began rubbing her hair. 'Why didn't you wake me at lunch-time? You shouldn't have gone off with him on your own.'

'I thought the girls would want to come too. There wouldn't have been room for all of us.'

'You put him on the spot, you know. It's highly unwise for a young male teacher to be seen driving around with a female pupil.'

'Nobody saw us.'

'You think! I bet the Kings did. Nigel never misses a trick. It'll be the talk of the street.'

'You shouldn't have let him stay the night in the first place. *That'll* be the talk of the street.'

Clare stopped kneading her head. She pushed the damp tangled mass of hair away from her face and leaned towards Lyn. 'As it happens, there's no harm done. But he obviously took it for granted that I'd be coming too. For God's sake, use your head! Trouble is, you don't realize how quickly you've grown up . . . '

'Mum . . . !'

36

'Men look at you, you know – not Matthew, I don't suppose – but other men.'

Lyn blocked her ears.

'They do. I've seen them – I need to tell you things. Don't tell me you know it all already . . . '

'I do. We've had it at school. A million times. Intercourse, contraception, abortion, miscellaneous diseases . . . '

Clare stood up. 'I'm talking about minds – and feelings. You don't get enough of that at school.' She leaned over and kissed Lyn on the forehead. 'Simon Reid rang up. There's some film he thought you'd want to see.'

'Now, there's a really sick mind! Can't stop thinking about bits of bodies!'

'Rubbish! Nice, normal boy!'

CHAPTER FIVE

It was English. Siân Watkins was in the doorway, watching the corridor. 'He's coming!'

There was a scuffle as people pushed their way into seats and got out their books. In a corner, Sarah Tucker gave her hair a last flick and tossed the brush into her bag. Lyn's heart hammered. Would he be remembering – the drumming rain, the steamy windows cocooning them, that sudden idea . . . had he had it too?

When she looked up, Matthew was standing at the front of the class, talking about John Donne. He was talking under his breath, rather quickly, and people were leaning forward over their desks, gripped by the fast flow of his words – like an underground stream, she thought, rumbling away, deep down, at any moment capable of bursting to the surface and sweeping you off.

I wouldn't care! Let him burst!

At that precise moment, he looked at her, full in the face. She gazed back. As his glance moved on, she picked up her pen and bent over her notebook. She waited for his voice to falter. But it didn't. Not once . . .

Didn't he feel as she did, then? Wasn't it the same for him? It couldn't be. At that second, she couldn't have carried on doing anything. She had been mesmerized . . . transfixed . . . pierced to the root.

CHAPTER SIX

At half-term, Matthew packed a small suitcase with clothes for the week and left for Hull. 'He's gone home,' said Clare. 'He thinks the world of his mother. She's been a widow for years. I get the impression she's one of those thrifty types that manage to make a go of things against all the odds. – There's a sister, too, you know. Something funny about her. I've a feeling she's not all there – not that he's said so, exactly . . . He sends the pair of them most of his money. I've got to admit, whatever else I find to say about her, Cardy's been a real brick about that. She doesn't charge him anything like the going rate for his room.' One of the students gave a laugh and remarked that perhaps she should move in with Cardy herself, but Clare wasn't listening. 'He's never lived away from home before,' she murmured. 'Not even when he was at university. I think he finds it quite hard, poor lad.'

'He's working up rather a soft spot for you,' the student ventured slyly.

'It's the mother in me!'

Both students cackled and Clare stood up and began collecting the plates. She was trying not to look pleased with herself, Lyn thought. You could tell she believed the students were right. A young man in his twenties had fallen for her! There was life in the old girl yet!

Beth had made it clear that she expected to see a lot of Lyn over half-term, to compensate for the hopeless situation at school. It was farcical now, she'd declared, with Lyn always dashing off to the library, even in her free time. It made you almost glad to be in all the div twos – unless Lyn was deliberately avoiding her, of course. Was something going on that she didn't know about?

On Tuesday, she found Lyn in Wellington Place. 'I've just been round to your place!' she said, juddering to a halt on her bicycle. She glanced across at Cardy's blank windows. 'What're you hanging round here for?'

'Nothing.' *Go away. Leave me to drag out the days. I don't want you. I don't want anyone . . .* His car wasn't there. She had known it wouldn't be . . .

'What's wrong?' Beth got off her bike and dragged it on to the pavement. 'Maybe it's glandular fever. Mum says people of our age are prone to it. She's on the look-out.'

'I'm perfectly OK.'

'Oh. Well, I feel ghastly!' Beth's voice dropped suddenly. 'Lyn, thank God there's you! I'm driving myself nuts over Mr Beech. Seriously. Sometimes I can't stop crying.'

'I thought you'd got over all that.'

Beth's knuckles whitened round her handle-bars. 'I dream about him. I spend my life waiting for English lessons. Don't let's go in yet. Let's walk. I don't want Clare to know. She'd think I ought to pull myself together. But I can't.'

Nor can I. They walked down Barnton Road, straight past forty-one and as far as the main road where the roar of traffic drowned all conversation. *Tell her. Tell her now! – But she wouldn't believe me, anyway. And, if she did, she wouldn't be able to bear it.*

They turned homeward, down a side road. 'It's only you that keeps me sane,' said Beth. 'I wish I mattered to you like that. It's all one way with us, isn't it? Why don't you tell me things too? You must get worried sometimes.'

'Not really,' said Lyn. 'I'm not the type.' A gust of wind hurtled down the street at them, swirling leaves and grit in their faces. Lyn's eyes stung. *Lies. Lies. Lies.*

Beth left early that day. She had been hoping to stay the night but, by tea-time, it was obvious that no one was going to ask her. Lyn excused herself from the supper table and, eventually, sent a message back with one of the students to say she'd been sick. She stuck her head round her bedroom door as Beth got ready to leave, and wandered into the front room to wave through the window. 'How are you?' said Clare curiously. 'Are you really sick?' They stood, side by side, watching Beth's forlorn form pedalling away, anorak flying out behind.

'It's not me you want to worry about,' said Lyn. 'It's her. She's still crazy about Matthew Beech. Did you ever say anything to him about her?'

'I decided against it,' said Clare. 'He doesn't come to me for advice on how to handle adolescent girls.'

'Oh.' Lyn turned away. 'What does he come to you for?'

'Nyl!'

'Hi.'

'I'm coming round. You look terrible. You've cycled straight past me twice this week. Did you know that?'

'Sorry.'

'You need taking out of yourself.'

'You can try.' *You won't succeed*. Lyn put the phone down. *You're not the one I want to see.*

Simon came the next morning. Lyn watched through the window as he chained his bike to the railings and chafed his cold hands. His trouser bottoms were stuffed in his socks; his hair was blown up in a peak at the front. Clare was right – nice and normal, i.e. Dead Boring. Except, to be fair, she hadn't thought that at first. Not till he started drooling over Sonia Cannelli.

'OK?' He stood in the hall, watching her button her coat and wind a long scarf round and round her neck. 'Don't strangle yourself.'

41

'Why not?'

They dug their hands deep in their pockets, sank their chins in their collars and trudged down to the canal. All along the towpath, the hedgerows were rigid with unthawed frost. Thick ice, white with a powdering of snow, had formed over the muddy water, and a small brown mongrel pattered along it ahead of them, occasionally losing its footing and looking alarmed.

'I still like you best,' said Simon. 'I wish you'd take me seriously.'

'I can't. I'm not free to. You might as well know. I'm hopelessly in love.'

'God!'

'By "hopelessly", I mean that the guy doesn't know, and I doubt he ever gives me a thought.'

'Ah!' Simon stooped to pick up a stone and crack it off across the ice. The mongrel yelped and took to its heels. 'Who is it? Or doesn't one ask?'

'No point, really.'

They strode on for another, silent, half-mile. 'Tell you what,' muttered Simon. 'Let's say we don't talk about anything personal.'

'What else is there?'

'This damn magazine, for a start. Beech is at me to rustle up at least half a dozen decent poems by the end of half-term!'

'Half a dozen's not many.'

'*Decent* ones. I've got mounds of crap. And that's a bloody pain, too! Everyone knows I'm poetry editor; I'll be lynched when the thing comes out, and people like Jason Freeman and John Pride aren't in!'

'Say Beech made the choice.'

'I can't. He keeps telling everyone the committee's entirely responsible.'

'So you're all hating him?'

'Well, actually, no. He's quite inspiring, in his way. It's his first job, you know. He's still dead enthusiastic.'

42

'I know. He talks to Mum. They've got quite friendly.'

'Oh! I see! Chatting up Clare, is he?'

'Don't be sick. Everyone's making cracks like that. You remember Cardy? . . . He's lodging with her, you know. She invited Mum round last week and seriously accused her of trying to seduce him. They had a hell of a row. God knows if they'll ever patch it up. I'm pig in the middle now, of course.'

Simon sighed. 'I don't really give a damn what Clare and Beech are up to, Nyl. I was going to give you a whole "spiel" about being over all that tits and bums rubbish. I'm into whole people now – the whole of you, for instance.'

CHAPTER SEVEN

Mrs Winifred Ryder had been head of the English Department at Gledhill for at least ten years. She was fifty-ish, short and stocky, with muscular calves and cropped hair. The pupils irreverently referred to her as 'Randy Ryder' because of the way she was rumoured to conduct herself at the staff Christmas party every year. Apparently, she marched round with a sprig of mistletoe, kissing anything that moved. Once, it was said, a hapless head-boy, arriving at the staff-room door on official business, had been hauled in and subjected to the full treatment! Mrs Ryder had been divorced for twenty years and everyone agreed she was 'gasping for it' – but no one said that, or anything like it, to her face. The most recalcitrant layabouts buckled down in her classes. Her line in sarcasm could leave you squirming for days.

'We *must* go to that!' Beth pointed at one of Mrs Ryder's notices on the general board in the entrance-hall. It was strikingly set out in black italic writing on purple card, and invited all members of the upper-school, who were interested in taking part, to attend a planning meeting for the end-of-term Christmas production. 'Mr Beech'll be helping with it. I don't care what I am as long as I'm something.'

'You ought to make a point of staying away,' said Lyn, 'to prove to yourself you're not completely in thrall!'

'Trouble is, I *am*!' Beth tossed her head. 'What the hell!'

In the end, they both went, along with a good hundred-and-fifty others. Mrs Ryder lorded it from the platform in the assembly hall, flanked by Matthew and a rather peaky young woman called Miss Clark. 'We're having readings,' announced Mrs Ryder. 'Not just from the Bible. An interesting selection . . . '

'*Whose* selection?' Simon muttered in Lyn's ear. He'd wangled a seat behind her, and kept embedding his toes in her rear to remind her of the fact.

'Tell him to get lost,' hissed Beth in her other ear. 'I can see what he's doing with his foot, you know. It's disgusting.'

' . . . of my own devising,' added Mrs Ryder.

'What did I tell you?' whispered Simon.

'Tell him to bugger off,' said Beth. 'You're always telling me you're not interested.'

'Shut up,' said Lyn. 'We're going to miss everything.'

'Everything' turned out to be that the readings would be accompanied by an elaborate mime for which music would be provided by the school orchestra. ('God!' groaned Simon. 'Count me out!') There would be lists on the main notice-board at the end of school for people to sign up if they wanted to be considered for a part or to offer their services behind the scenes.

'I'll do props or something,' Lyn murmured. So far, Matthew didn't appear to have spotted her in the crowd. Presumably, he wasn't trying to spot her. It was the first day back after half-term. His car had reappeared outside Cardy's yesterday – she could almost pinpoint the very minute, as she'd spent the whole day checking. On her ninth time round the block it hadn't been there, and, on the tenth, it had. That put it at about four thirty-five. She had hoped he would call round to see Clare – he had sent her a postcard of an ancient pub called The Cat and Fiddle, telling her the beer wasn't a patch on The Bell's – but he hadn't come. At her usual time, Clare had departed for The Bell and, when she came back, Lyn was in bed. She was pretty sure Clare had come home alone but at breakfast she hadn't asked.

45

'Props and wardrobe is Miss Clark,' Beth was saying. 'That'll be a real drag. Try for a part. *He*'s in charge of that. I'm going to.'

'Heaven help us if he turns you down.'

'He won't.' Beth smiled to herself. 'I know he won't. I think he's beginning to value me.'

As she strolled home Lyn felt herself oddly disconcerted. Beth's words, with their strange new certainty of tone, kept echoing in her head. How on earth could he *value* Beth? What could possibly make her think so? Had he said something to her? Did he say things to lots of people?

That evening, she was sullen and long-faced at supper. 'Hormones?' said Clare.

'Shut up!' Lyn glanced at the students.

'Don't be silly,' said Clare. 'Natural function – nothing to be embarrassed about. All girls together.'

'You're embarrassing everyone,' said Lyn coldly. 'And *you're* not a girl, anyway. Not by any stretch of the imagination.'

For the next three days, Beth prattled constantly about the auditions. 'You should have signed up for a try, Lyn. Everyone's having a go. Mr Beech'll be fantastic. He's great on the magazine committee. Hasn't Sexy Simon told you?' Lyn tried not to listen. Like hell was she going to hang round Matthew Beech, licking his feet so he'd give her a part! He'd made a complete fool of her, pretending he thought she was special, making her think there was something . . . She'd wasted weeks of her life on him already.

'Try for a part, Nylly,' said Simon. 'Give us something worth watching.'

'I thought you said you'd given up that mindless gawping.'

Simon blinked. '*Geez*! Who *is* this bloke? He's really screwing you up.'

'Far from it! – He still doesn't even know.'

'Tell him then. For God's sake, let's get the whole thing

started. Sooner it starts, sooner it fizzles. I can't wait for ever, Nyl. The day could come when you turn to my ever-loving arms and find them closed round someone else. Ever thought of that?'

'Put it in a poem,' said Lyn, 'and stick it in your magazine.'

On the day of the auditions, she kept clear of the hall. Beth, to her sheer joy, was given the part of the Angel Gabriel. 'Everyone's jealous as hell. They're in a huddle, saying I'm useless.'

'It's a mime. You probably got that part because of your ballet.'

Beth nodded. 'Mr Beech says there's a massive dance when I first appear to the Virgin Mary.'

'Who's he picked for her?'

'He hasn't! Everyone's on tenterhooks.'

'It'll need to be someone with real class. Try finding that at Gledhill.'

'You know,' Beth said slowly, 'you're really vile these days. Just piss off. You're not wrecking my day.'

But, as it turned out there was nothing she, or anyone else, could do to prevent just that. At the end of the afternoon, someone brought Lyn a message from Mr Beech, asking her to see him outside the staff-room. Beth watched from the end of the corridor, chewing her nails angrily. What now? How had he got time for Lyn in the midst of auditioning and casting?

'Lyn, I'd like you to take the part of the Virgin,' Matthew was saying, twenty yards away. 'It's a pity you didn't sign up for a trial. You're the obvious choice.'

'There'll be an uproar,' said Lyn. 'People are hanging round the notice-board downstairs, waiting to see who you've chosen.'

'I've chosen you.'

'Oh.' Lyn tried to smile. She gulped uncomfortably. 'I wouldn't have to be padded in front, would I – to look pregnant? I wouldn't have to carry a doll?'

47

'It's mime. You have to convey everything by the way you move. You must make us believe you're pregnant. And you must make us believe there's something in your arms.'

'Not *"something"*.' She gave a croaky laugh. 'Not any old thing! God, himself, isn't it?'

He laughed too. 'Are you all right, Lyn? Are you happy?'

She nodded.

'It's me, then. I keep sensing some sort of barrier. It's hard to teach people once they've turned negative. It's hard to get through. Don't take the part if you don't want it.'

'I do want it.' With no warning, Lyn's legs were turning to jelly. 'I wanted it all along.' She bolted before he could see the tears in her eyes.

After that, she was hated. She revelled in it. She was suffering for *him*. He was worth it.

'People wonder why he had to pick you,' said Beth, grudgingly making peace after about a week. 'I wonder, too. You don't look specially virginal.'

'You're jealous!'

'I'm not. I've got a perfectly good part of my own. A vital role. Nothing would have happened if Gabriel hadn't said his piece.'

'Course it would!' Lyn giggled. 'Mary would still have had the baby. Nothing would have changed that.'

'Well, she wouldn't have known whose it was, would she? Nobody would.'

'It's only a story.'

'It's true,' said Beth. 'You shouldn't be Mary if you don't believe it. He should have given the part to someone who at least goes to church.' Slowly the pinched look was creeping over her face. 'People think you're his favourite, Lyn. But I don't think he has them, do you?'

'No,' said Lyn. Being loved was more than being a 'favourite', someone's toy to be picked up and put down on a whim. And she *was* loved. He'd told her that – twice – not in so many words, but . . .

In rehearsals, she moved only for him – every gesture a wooing. She could see from his face that he understood. His eyes never left her. She saw herself through them – her white form, threading its way through angel hosts, shepherds, wise men, to the stable. At the foot of the manger, she knelt and gazed into a pile of straw that Cardy had dug out of an old tea-chest in her attic. 'What do you see?' Matthew asked her once, at the end of a rehearsal. 'What's in your mind?'

You. 'Nothing. I listen to the words. The readers are brilliant, aren't they?'

'Do you believe the story? You look as if you do.'

That day, Lyn returned back-stage, to look for a belt she had lost. Through the curtains, she could hear Mrs Ryder's voice, sharp with impatience. 'You'll have to get a grip on yourself, Matthew. You're too fascinated by half. You aren't here to ask her about herself and her beliefs. You're here to teach her English and she's here to be taught.'

'I know her mother,' came Matthew's voice, placatory. 'She's had some sort of theatrical training. Lyn's obviously inherited her talent – a hundredfold!'

'I wasn't born yesterday,' muttered Mrs Ryder. 'I hate children that look interesting. They never are.'

CHAPTER EIGHT

Lyn stood in the centre of the Hastingses' sitting-room, sipping at a glass of Mrs Hastings's fruit punch and acknowledging, rather dreamily, the paeans of praise ringing out all round. She was separate inside her circle, it struck her, and Beth and Matthew were separate outside it. She could see Beth, lurking in a corner, masking poisonous thoughts with a fixed smile. She'd been fuming because Lyn was getting all the attention, even though it was the Hastingses who were actually giving the party. They had decided to hold 'Open House' to celebrate the last night of the play as well as Beth's and Lyn's sixteenth birthdays, both of which fell that week.

She watched Beth stuff a sausage in her mouth and whisper something to her mother. Mrs Hastings responded rapidly, and then ducked out of sight under the table. There was a slight smell of singeing in the air. Seconds earlier, the head of a match had shot, flaming, into the air, and vanished. People had stamped energetically on the carpet and said: 'Got it!' But, clearly, Mrs Hastings remained unconvinced.

Matthew was leaning against a wall, eating a vol-au-vent, his plate held under his chin to catch the crumbs. Mrs Ryder had sidled up beside him and was chatting earnestly. She was flushed with excitement, and kept patting his arm. Perhaps they're talking about me, Lyn thought – agreeing, with everyone else, that I was brilliant! She grinned into her glass. Mr Hastings had just breathed his own accolade in her ear, puffing cigar smoke and lapsing into a flat, drawling accent she'd heard him use only once or twice before. 'Call me "merry" if you like, Miss – I've always credited you with an extra little something and now I'm proved right! Real talent there! You'll leave the rest standing, believe me.' He had backed off and continued on his round, litre bottles of white wine in either hand. Over his shoulder, Lyn had met Matthew's glance.

'You did ever so well tonight,' someone else said. It was Miss Clark, in a red dress with a tight black belt. She had black patent shoes and a matching bag and reminded Lyn of a Christmas cracker about to go off with a bang. 'You're like me, Lyn,' she said, confidingly. 'A loner. You've had people milling round you all night, but you still give the impression of being on your own.'

'I've got friends,' said Lyn. There was Beth. And Simon Reid was here somewhere. He had been easily the best of the readers, filling the hall with resonant, rich tones she hadn't known he possessed. 'They're in the other room.'

'Oh, I'm sure they are,' said Miss Clark. 'But you don't feel compelled to join them. You don't need to socialize, just for the sake of it.'

Miss Clark's wine glass was shaking slightly in her hand, Lyn noticed. The hem of the red dress was quivering. 'Don't you like parties, Miss Clark?'

'Could you hold this a minute?' Miss Clark thrust her glass suddenly at Lyn and turned away.

'Do you need a hanky?' Lyn watched in alarm as Miss Clark's shoulders began to heave.

'It's such a *hellish* department,' whimpered Miss Clark. 'I shouldn't be saying this to you, I know, but Mrs Ryder treats me like a moron. I'm always "wardrobe and make-up". And now there's Mr Beech I'm certainly never going to be anything else. I'll have to resign.'

Lyn took a quick sip from Miss Clark's glass. The wine

was cold and tart. 'Oh, don't, Miss Clark. No one likes Mrs Ryder. Everyone likes you.'

'I find that hard to believe.'

'It's true. Of course, some of the girls are dotty on Mr Beech at the moment. But they still like you.'

'And I like them.' Miss Clark took a number of deep breaths and turned back into the room. 'It's just Win. She's so domineering. If you're in with her, you're all right, but, if you're not, heaven help you!'

'Is Mr Beech in with her, then?'

'Of course. Haven't you spotted them, whispering away over there, all cheek by jowl, having their little secrets and their little sniggers?'

'He's got no taste.'

'Well, he knows which side his bread's buttered, doesn't he? I don't say I blame him. Heavens, Lyn! Why am I telling you all this? I must say, you know, it's very hard to believe you're only just sixteen. I wonder if I'll get you in an A-level class next year. That would be fun. We'd get on . . . '

'You've changed your mind, then,' said Lyn, 'about resigning. You've cheered up.'

Miss Clark took her glass and moved away. 'What was all that about?' demanded Beth, taking her place. 'Mum says Clark's been crying.'

'She has.'

'What about?'

'I don't think I'm supposed to say.'

Beth glared, then exploded. 'God! I can't stand you. It's only adults that think you're so great, you know. Everyone else says you stink.'

Lyn went in search of her coat. In the normal way, she would have expected to stay the night with the Hastingses, but they were having visitors next day and Mrs Hastings had already started on a bit of surreptitious tidying-up. In the hall, there was a crush of people heading for the door, clutching costumes, and grease-proof bags full of left-overs.

'How about some lifts?' bellowed Mr Hastings. 'Can't have youngsters drifting into the streets at this time of night.'

'I can take a load,' said Matthew. He stretched out and tapped Lyn's shoulder. 'I can take you, Lyn.'

He took four altogether. They piled noisily into the car and started calling out garbled directions as he revved the engine. Through the window, Lyn caught sight of Simon, by the gate with a couple of friends. The other two were lighting cigarettes, but Simon's eyes were fixed on her. He looked pale in the lamplight. She waved, but he didn't wave back.

Matthew seemed to be dropping everyone else off first. Lyn fell silent as the car emptied. She was sitting in the front seat beside him, her hands clasped round a bag of Hastings sausage-rolls. 'For God's sake,' he whispered, as the last person disappeared up an alley, leaving them alone, 'stop squashing that revolting bag.'

They drove on, silent again, until, just before Barnton Road, he turned suddenly into a cul-de-sac and pulled up. 'Well?'

Overhead, a street-lamp glared down on them. She hung her head. 'Well what?'

He turned, one arm resting along the back of his seat, the other across the top of the wheel. 'What are we going to do?'

'What do you mean?'

He put a finger under her chin and lifted her face. 'You know perfectly well. You know where we've been, this last four weeks or so – what's been going on. Each rehearsal, each performance, was for me, wasn't it? A ritual. I'm won, Lyn. I'm yours. I was long before.'

She couldn't speak. His black head was coming closer, blocking out the lamp . . . It wasn't like a first kiss. 'We've been doing this all our lives,' he breathed. 'We must have been!' He drew back, holding one of her hands to his mouth, murmuring into her fingers. 'It feels so right, doesn't it? It *is* right.'

'I don't know. I don't know anything.'

He took her in his arms again. 'You know everything. By pure instinct. It's true – do you believe me?'

'Almost. When we're like this. But I don't know what I'll think when I get home. I'll be scared.'

He held her face in front of his. In the shadow, his eyes seemed lost in their deep, dark sockets. 'Remember me.'

'Kiss me,' she said. 'I'm scared already.'

She had hoped they would all be in bed when she got back, but a light was on in the kitchen, and people were talking. 'In here!' sang Clare. She and the lodgers were sitting round the table with cans of lager. They weren't bothering with glasses. There were a few peanuts and a lot of salt left in the bottom of a bowl. 'How did you get home?'

'Got a lift.'

'Did everything go all right?'

'Fine. You could have come to the party, you know. There were quite a few parents there. In fact, it looked a bit odd, you staying away, when it was partly to celebrate my birthday.'

'It's you the Hastingses like. I embarrass them.' Clare grinned. 'Perhaps they should join forces with Cardy!'

'Don't be silly. You were definitely invited.'

'She didn't want to cramp Matthew's style,' whispered one of the students. 'She didn't want to inhibit him, doing his teacher bit.'

'She wouldn't have inhibited him in the least.'

The student looked from Clare to Lyn and back again. 'She might as well know, mightn't she? – The fact is, Lyn, your English teacher is totally smitten with dear Clare! He's like a basilisk when she's around – just stares and stares.'

'He's like that with everyone,' said Lyn.

'Not me, I'm glad to say!' The student sniggered. 'I find him extremely creepy!'

'Take no notice,' said Clare. 'She's having you on.'

She was looking pleased with herself again, Lyn thought – flattered by what the student had said, secretly inclined to think she was right. She took some of the peanuts and went away to her bedroom. 'Remember me.' She undressed and huddled in bed, in the cold and dark. She felt his kiss again, the pull of his arms, the smoothness of his shoulder where she'd burrowed for warmth. Once, she had wondered if she would really want all that!

Only four days of term remained, and only two English lessons. In both, Matthew's gaze was clear and untroubled. *You'll have to send for me. I can't hang around, starstruck, in corridors.*

'Matthew's going away for the whole of Christmas,' Clare said, the evening before the last day. 'Isn't that a drag? I thought we'd be able to have him to ourselves when the students go away. They're so immature with their endless little digs.'

'Maybe it's one of them he fancies,' said Lyn. 'I suppose that's quite likely, really.'

Clare put down her book. She swung her feet off the sofa and fixed Lyn with a straight look. 'Amazing as you obviously find it, the reason Matthew comes round here is that he and I have a particular rapport.' She waved the book in the air. 'He's trying to educate me. We talk about literature the whole time! People in the pub think we're bats!'

'You'll have to speak to Beth about that one,' said Lyn witheringly. 'He did *Sons and Lovers* with Div Two.'

The next day, she did hang around in corridors. Once, near the staff-room, he glanced at her but didn't stop. By lunch-time, she had decided to shake Beth off at the end of school and lie in wait for him on his way home. How could he contemplate vanishing for weeks without a word – as if four nights ago hadn't happened? What was she supposed to think? She had told him she'd be scared. Didn't he care?

To her surprise, at the end of the afternoon, Beth disappeared voluntarily. She went off to the cloakroom and didn't come back. Lyn packed her bag fast, grabbed her hockey-stick from the rack by the gym, and hurried out of school. Twenty yards up the road, a lorry was parked on the other side. She crossed over and sheltered behind it. School had finished early but the usual Christmas revelries were in progress in the staff-room. She was in for a long wait.

It was cold. She leaned into the side of the lorry, out of the wind. Every now and again, she peered round the front, to check the stream of pupils trudging up the opposite pavement towards the main road. She didn't see Beth and, as the stream thinned to a trickle and eventually dried up altogether, she concluded she had missed her. By half-past four, it was dark. School had been out for more than an hour and her feet were numb blocks. She left her belongings in a heap and headed back to the gate. The staff-room lights would be blazing. She might catch glimpses of what was going on inside . . .

The quadrangle lay benighted. Across the other side, she could make out the shadowy bulk of the unlit science block. To the left, the music wing seemed deserted too. She set off down a narrow passage to the right that led to the old cycle-sheds. It was a short cut between buildings that would bring her out at what was known as 'Baby Quad', otherwise only approached by a special visitors' gate. There was a small ornamental pool there, frozen solid now, and a sundial donated by former pupils. The staff-room overlooked it. She sneaked along in the gloom, expecting soon to come upon lighted windows and sounds of hilarity.

The open-sided cycle-sheds loomed ahead on the left. No one used them for bikes any more. There was a better place in the big quad. Now, the gardener and caretaker stored bits of equipment here – old tennis-nets and goal-posts and coils of perished hose. Lyn froze suddenly. *Voices*! Somewhere ahead. She strained. A loose sheet of corrugated roofing banged in the wind. Then . . . the voices again . . . murmuring . . .

56

Lyn held her breath. In the shadows of the first shed, two outlines slowly inked themselves in . . . *Matthew* . . . She pressed against the wall, edging closer. Yes, definitely. With *Beth*! She rubbed her eyes hard. She blinked and stared desperately . . . *Matthew and Beth*!

CHAPTER NINE

'Oh, it's you, Lyn. I thought you'd abandoned me,' said Cardy, peering round her front door. She was clutching a dusty Christmas wreath and looked old suddenly. 'I'm getting my decorations out.'

'I was wanting to see Mr Beech,' said Lyn, stepping inside. The hall was dank and dingy. No lights upstairs. He'd gone already, she guessed, spirited himself away while she was trudging the icy streets, tempest-tossed.

'He left half an hour ago,' sighed Cardy. 'Didn't you see his car was missing? He won't be back for three weeks.'

'You'll miss him.'

Cardy nodded.

'Look, I'll give you a hand with your decorations.'

Cardy nodded again. She took Lyn along to the kitchen, where a large card stood on the mantelpiece. It was of the Virgin and Child. Mary's face was smooth and oval, eyes closed in bliss as she held the infant to her cheek. 'Matthew gave it to me before he left,' she said, taking it down. 'It's like you in that play.'

'D'you think so?' But it had all been an act – for him. 'He's a brilliant teacher, Cardy. He can make you believe anything.' She sat down and poked about in the box of decorations. 'You need a tree. These things'd look nice.'

Cardy brought out a shiny tin of biscuits. 'He gave me these too,' she said, breaking into a wan smile. 'Have one, Lyn. There's no point me saving them till Christmas Day.'

For the Day, Clare had bought a turkey. 'Damn silly, really!' she said. 'Twelve whole pounds of prime fowl! We'll be sick of it.'

'We could invite Cardy. Bury the hatchet.'

'She thinks I'm over-the-top already, without sitting her down in front of a bird the same size as she is! Anyway, she wouldn't be able to stop lecturing me.'

On Christmas Eve, they hung paper-chains the length of the hall, zig-zagging to and fro across the ceiling. 'Gran didn't like these,' said Lyn, standing on a chair to pin one over the doorway of the empty bedroom. 'She said they were tawdry.' That night, she stood chopping onions for the stuffing, letting the tears stream down her face.

'Those tears look real,' said Clare, peering at her anxiously. 'Are you all right? Why don't you ask a friend round tomorrow afternoon, or something? Oh, I meant to tell you, Simon rang. At least, I assume it was him – he didn't say.'

'When?'

'The day you broke up. I didn't know where you were. Turned out you'd called in at Cardy's, remember? I thought it was Matthew at first – wanting me. Sounded just like him!'

'*Oh*!' Lyn tossed the onions into the mixture and stirred furiously. She stood back and brushed at her tears with the back of her hand. Inside, everything was bubbling and fizzing. *Could* it have been . . . ? It *must* have been . . . While she was trudging . . . weeping . . . cursing . . . he *had* tried to reach her!

The bubbling lasted all night and on into Christmas morning. 'You're volatile!' remarked Clare. 'Lead yesterday, and today I think you'd float away if I opened the door.'

59

They sat down to lunch at about two. Clare had started with sherry at twelve – to bring her own spirits in line with Lyn's, she said – before calculating that the turkey had at least another ninety minutes to go. After that, in some befuddlement, she had confused the bread- and rum-sauces, tipping liberal quantities of essence into the wrong one. 'Don't worry,' said Lyn, 'I won't notice the difference.'

'I wish the phone would ring.' Clare thrust her hair back from her brow and began to carve. 'I just wish someone in the whole world would want to wish us a happy Christmas. My God! I'm seeing double! D'you mind a finger instead of a wing?'

'I bet some of the people from The Players will phone later.'

'Not them. I want *him* to phone.'

'Who?'

'Matthew.'

'He'll be sitting at some bare board of a table in the wilds of Yorkshire, won't he?'

'With the mother and the sister. A joyless little trio. Why didn't I tell him to ask them down here? He could have stayed on at Cardy's. They could have stayed with us. We could all have dug into this damn thing together.' Clare jabbed the carving-fork deep into the turkey's breast and left it throbbing there. Juices streamed silently down its crisp skin into the bottom of the dish.

'What's wrong?' whispered Lyn. 'I like it being us. Anyway, he'd never have come. That's fantasy. None of them would have wanted to.'

'You don't know.' Clare began to sob. 'He's a friend of mine. You don't seem to realize.'

'Well, they probably invite relatives – grannies and aunts and things. That's all part of Christmas, isn't it, for most people?'

'*O-o-o-oh*!' Clare let out a lingering wail. 'Why isn't Gran still here? She ought to be sitting where you are, boring us

rigid with tales of the "good old days" – Uncle Tom breaking his tooth on a silver threepenny-bit, real candles on a
real tree . . . '

'Oh, Mum!' With a pang of guilt, Lyn realized she hadn't
given Gran a thought all day. She was hugging her bliss to
herself, brimming with her own secret happiness. 'I know
how you feel.'

Later, in a spirit of charity, she scurried off through the
sleet to spend half an hour with Cardy. 'I knew you'd
come,' Cardy said, flooding her with guilt again, as it was
by sheer fluke that the idea had crossed her mind. 'I saved
this for you.' She set a match to a slim, white candle, hand-
painted with ivy leaves. 'Matthew sent it through the post.'

Lyn kicked off her shoes and stretched her toes towards
the fire. The candle-flame flickered and then grew very still
and tall. 'I'm so happy, Cardy. Are you?'

That night, Nigel and Joan King came to supper. Lyn had
returned from Cardy's to find Clare, barefoot on the doorstep, issuing the invitation to Nigel as he chipped ice from
his path. 'You've lost your wits, Mum!' she had muttered,
chivvying her back inside.

'I'm old.' Clare's eyelids were puffy. 'I look a fright.
You're the beauty.' She dropped into a chair and covered
her face with her hands. 'My office is a tip. I thought I'd
clear it out. I tore half the stuff down, then I kept getting
visions of Gran so I started sticking it all back up again. Oh,
Lynny, I wish you hadn't gone out. I made a silly phone
call.'

'Who to?'

'Can't you guess?' Clare raised bleary eyes.

'Not Matthew! Oh, Mum! What on earth did you say?'

'I got his mother. I just said "Happy Christmas". Then he
spoke to me as well. Oh, dear, I'm afraid I'm pickled . . . '

But, by the evening, she was composed and elegant, in a

long, black dress and a peacock shawl. 'I must say you've improved since I last saw you!' said Nigel, giving her a nudge as she gathered up the plates. 'You'd had a few by the look of you!'

'So've you,' hooted his wife, 'by the sound of you!'

Clare smiled absently. She swept away with the plates and began deftly collecting items for the next course. Lyn watched her, spellbound. She was a phoenix – forever rising from her own ashes! She was all Gran had said she was. In her downfallings and uprisings was pure artistry!

Beth was still stirring. Lyn could hear her in the dark, tossing and turning in the scratchy old sleeping-bag. She'd been away all Christmas, skiing in Austria, but, as soon as she'd come back, she'd asked herself round. 'I've got something to tell you,' she'd muttered over the phone.

At last!

The next day, Lyn had watched for her from the sitting-room window. She had arrived bearing gifts, a carved wooden squirrel for Lyn and an edelweiss brooch for Clare. 'You said you had something to tell me.'

'Oh, later. No hurry.'

Lyn had waited all day . . .

'Are you still awake, Lynny?'

Lyn raised herself up on an elbow. She could see the lurking mass of Beth and her bedding, down near the floor. 'What is it?'

Beth gulped and coughed out her words in a hard lump. 'Well, you know how I feel about Mr Beech? At the end of term, I got him to meet me.'

'Meet you?'

'At the old bike-sheds near Baby Quad.'

'What for?'

'I told him, Lyn. I told him how I felt.'

Lyn whistled through her teeth.

'He was wonderful. He really was. I felt marvellous, at first. But now it's got bad again. I don't know what I'm going to do. I feel as if . . . don't laugh . . . I want to *marry* him. I really do. If I can't have him I don't want *anyone . . . ever*!'

Lyn lay down again, eyes wide open. *Put her out of her misery.* 'He's probably got someone already, Beth. Don't you think so? Up North, maybe.'

'He patted my hand. I can't tell you how it felt. D'you think he likes me, Lyn? D'you think it's possible?'

'Of course, he likes you! I expect he likes all of us . . . ' *Tell her. No lies.*

'Specially, I mean.'

'No.'

'No?'

'Not specially. It's more than his job's worth.'

'What if I changed schools?'

Lyn reached out and switched on her bedside light. Beth was sitting, shrunken and pale, hugging her knees. She blinked. 'What did you do that for?'

'It was getting unreal.' *He loves me. That feels unreal too. Stop blinking. Stop looking demented. It's true.* 'You were getting carried away.'

'You've got to understand, Lyn. There's got to be someone on my side.'

63

CHAPTER TEN

Two more days... One more day... *Now*! As she approached the corner for the fourth time, Lyn's heart banged at her ribs, hard as a cricket ball. She rounded the bend... *No*... Round the block again, and again, and... Ah! It was there – the Mini, with Matthew half in and half out, tugging at luggage – she faltered, then spun on her heel and walked swiftly home. 'He's back,' she told Clare. 'You'll probably see him down at the pub tonight.'

Clare looked up from her ironing and pulled a face. 'I'll have to apologize for that awful phone call. How embarrassing! That's if he manages to escape from Cardy, of course. She'll want him all to herself tonight.'

She won't get him! When no one was looking, Lyn slipped out of the house and along the road to the public phone. 'It's me!' Cardy had called up the stairs to him. She had heard him thumping down, and muffled whispers. 'I had to sound all foreign for Cardy so she didn't recognize me.'

'Ah!'

'Sorry, if you're all disappointed.'

'Not at all.'

'Is she still hanging round?'

'That's right.'

'I saw you unpacking your car this afternoon. I wanted to talk, but I thought she'd be watching. Can we meet tonight?'

'That would be nice.'

'Mum'll go along to the pub about nine. I'll come to the end of the road as soon as she's gone. Can you pick me up?'

It was a clear night, very cold. The rear lights of the small car were glowing at the end of the street. Lyn ran. She was panting by the time she pulled open the door and climbed in. He moved off quickly, glancing at her just once.

'Where are we going?'

'Somewhere quiet.' He took the main road out of town and, after a few miles, turned off down a winding lane.

'I had to see you.' She was shivering. 'I couldn't just leave it, after last time. I tried to catch you before you went away. I saw you with Beth in the school bike-sheds. I didn't know what to think. She's told me now.'

He turned to her quickly, then back to the road. 'Shhh.' He put a finger to his lips. 'I'll explain.'

They were entering a village, huddled and dimly lit. He nosed the car through narrow streets not meant for cars, between low-roofed cottages. No one saw them. 'I wish there was only us in the whole world,' said Lyn. 'Things would be easy, then.'

They came out, suddenly, among bare, moonlit fields, stretching away on either side. Matthew swung the car in at a gate and switched everything off. The white blur of his face loomed nearer, seeking her out. 'Beth sent me a note. It appeared in my pigeon-hole the day after the party. Unsigned. I thought it was from you. I thought it was you I was going to meet. Then I tried to phone, but you weren't there . . . '

'Beth's besotted about you.'

'She was.'

'Still is.'

He took her hand. '*Lyn* . . !' He held it to his cheek. 'I've waited for this.'

'Oh, so have I. You know how you said last time that you were mine? – I'm yours, too. I would have told you then, only I don't think I had realized. Not completely.'

65

'You were scared. Afterwards, I was scared for you. So young to be in love. I've wondered all Christmas how you were bearing it.'

They found a way of sitting along the back seat together. He unbuttoned his thick jacket and took her inside it. 'You smell of Cardy's house already,' she whispered, 'and you've only been back a few hours!'

'You smell of you.' He untied her hair and buried his face in it. 'I could lose myself in that smell.'

'One of us is trembling.'

'Both of us, I think.'

They laughed shakily. She drew back an inch. 'I don't want it ever to end.'

'No time . . . no place . . . no end . . . '

'What do you mean?' She strained to make out his features in the dark. 'There'll have to be times and places, won't there? People will find out otherwise. – It wouldn't be allowed, would it? I mean, with you being on the staff . . . '

He didn't reply. After a while, he pulled a wallet from his pocket and took out a photograph, switching on the small car light for her to see by. 'My mother,' he said, 'and sister.'

'Oh.' Lyn settled back against his shoulder and peered at the picture curiously. 'She's like you, your sister. She's got your eyes.'

'Has she? She's almost exactly the same age as you.'

'Oh.'

'Physically, that is. Mentally, she's about six.' He took the photo back and tucked it out of sight again.

'Matthew . . . I don't know what to say.'

He stroked a finger along her lower lip. 'Don't say anything. I was just thinking, that's all. She's in another world, you see. No rules for her. In that way, she's better off than us.'

'Wonderful! Fantastic!' sang Beth at break. 'He kept glancing at me all lesson. I know he was remembering . . . '

Lyn emptied her pencil-case into her lap and began sharpening her pencils, one by one. 'You're inventing things. You'll work yourself into a state again.'

'Who cares? It's bliss!'

The previous evening, Lyn had crept in at half-past eleven. Clare had been in the kitchen, regaling the new lodgers with tales of some of the wilder exploits of The Players. 'Sometimes a teacher from Lyn's school comes along to meetings, doesn't he, Lyn? – an innocent by the name of Matthew Beech. He needs bringing out of himself. I think you two would do him a lot of good.' She cocked an eyebrow at Lyn. 'Don't you think so, Lyn? Don't you think Matthew might benefit from the attentions of Jackie and Anna?'

'I suppose he might. He wasn't there, then, tonight?'

'No. I'm very sad, but not at all surprised, to say he wasn't. Cardy will have sunk her claws in as far as the bone. Heaven knows when the poor lamb will escape!'

Lyn grinned at the lodgers and poured herself a drink of water to take off to bed. Clare was obviously in fine form. She had totally lost track of the time. 'I'll say goodnight, then.'

'Not so fast.' Clare's eyes narrowed suddenly and she jerked herself upright in her chair. 'Where, if it's not too much to ask, have you been till this time of night?'

'Nowhere.'

'Ah! "Nowhere." '

The students shifted uncomfortably, and one of them began collecting up coffee mugs and taking them over to the sink.

'I had to meet someone.'

'Who?'

'No one you know, Mum.'

'Oh, I see.' Clare lit a cigarette and puffed at it once or twice. 'You're sixteen years old – just. Over my dead body do you go waltzing off into the night on mystery dates.'

'It'll be a boy-friend, Mrs Mellor,' whispered one of the girls. 'I can remember trying to keep my first boy-friend a secret. It's only natural.'

'Is that so?' Clare waved both girls away and, when she was alone with Lyn, slapped the table-top loudly. '*Who*?'

'I don't ask where you've been – though, from the look of you, I hardly need to. If I have got a boy-friend – *if* – I'm certainly not going to start telling you about him – specially in front of those *twits*!' Lyn stormed off to her bedroom and sat, shaking, on the edge of her bed. *Attack, attack, attack.* The only way. Clare mustn't find out . . .

'Lynny . . . ' It was half an hour later. Clare shuffled limply into the room and flopped on a cushion. 'I'm a hopeless mother, you don't need to tell me, but I'm trying, you know. I'm sure you ought to tell me where you've been.'

Lyn carried on brushing her hair. Clare wasn't drunk any more. She was anxious and sad. 'Don't fuss, Mum!' Lyn couldn't bear to look at her. 'I want a bit of privacy, that's all. We can't be in each other's pockets all the time, telling each other everything.'

'Am I hanging on to you, then?' Clare paused to consider it. 'Am I a weight round your neck?'

'No, course you're not. I'm just thinking how it might get.'

Clare nodded slowly. 'So, that's all. You just want to be more independent. You're not hiding something?'

'No, I'm not. There's nothing to worry about.'

'On the Bible?'

Lyn's stomach knotted. The childhood 'swear' that meant the end of all lies: 'On the Bible.'

Clare got to her feet and wandered towards the door. 'It's quite hard not to worry. We get letters from school, you know – drugs and all sorts . . . '

He was different in class. No more looks that left her

breathless, pierced through! Too dangerous, too risky, too much to hide. One night, he came back from The Bell with Clare. They sat, the three of them, in the sitting-room, drinking coffee. 'Lyn had a mystery meeting the other night, Matthew,' said Clare. 'What do you think of that?'

He cleared his throat and looked across at her, then back at Clare. 'I suppose it's a good thing. You need to experiment with relationships when you're young. I didn't do enough of that when I was at school.'

'Do you do enough of it now?' said Clare. 'That's what I ask myself!' She pealed with laughter and went off to give a message to one of the students.

'I was with *you*!' whispered Lyn. 'I couldn't tell her.'

'Meet me again, Lynny. Tomorrow. We've got to talk.'

The next night, there was a warm package on the passenger seat. Lyn opened it and fed hot chips into his mouth as he drove. 'What did you say to Clare this time?'

'She's at the pub. I'll probably be back first.'

'Good!' At the first quiet spot, he slowed down and pulled the car over on to a rough verge. 'Everything between us is true, Lyn. I can't bear to prop it up with lies. I hate that.' He drew her towards him. 'I love you. No lies.'

'I love you too.' She was puzzled by his vehemence. 'We probably don't need to lie all that much.'

It wasn't till she got home again that she realized that not saying anything was a type of lie. He knew that. They were silently lying to everyone all the time.

'Wake up, for God's sake!' grumbled Simon. 'Don't you see the rest of us any more? Don't we count?'

'Sorry?'

'It's going OK now, is it, you and this guy?'

She nodded. 'I suppose so.'

He grimaced. 'Just for old times' sake, you wouldn't

69

fancy going over some of these poems with me, would you?
I'd like another opinion.'

'Bring them round some time.'

He gripped her wrist. 'How long's it going to last?'

'Don't ask. Bring the poems.'

There was something the matter with Clare. She came
home from the pub blind drunk one night. Lyn watched
from the sitting-room window as she lurched along the
pavement on Matthew's arm. Outside the house, she
plucked at his sleeve and turned her face up to be kissed.
Lyn fled. She was standing, motionless, in the hall as they
came in. Clare blinked at her with large dopey eyes.

'Mr Beech has given me something wildly potent to
drink! I can only assume he's got hugely improper
designs!' She flung her coat over the hall chair and floun-
dered down the passage towards the kitchen.

Matthew reached for Lyn's arm but she slipped past him
into her bedroom and locked the door. 'Lyn!' He tapped
lightly with his fingers.

'*Liar!*'

He went on tapping but she didn't open the door and, at
last, he went away. Later, she heard the desperate flapping
of Clare's feet in the hall and up and down the stairs.
'Mum?' She poked her head out into the passage but there
was no sign of Clare and the front door was gaping wide.

'Tut, tut!' commented Nigel King from his own doorstep
as she came out to investigate. 'Why is a classy lady, like
your mum, running after a little runt like that?'

Lyn drew herself up in fury. 'Piss off, Mr King!' Then she
set off after Clare who was swaying uncertainly along the
pavement some way ahead. Matthew was nowhere in
sight.

CHAPTER ELEVEN

'That was inexcusable,' said Clare. It was breakfast time and she was sitting at the table, pale but collected – no trace of last night's rag-tag hair and wry mouth.

'I thought you'd be hung over backwards!'

'I don't expect you actually to believe this, at the moment,' Clare went on, 'but that's IT! When it comes to being half-carried home by a boy in his twenties then I know it's time to call a halt!' She shook a cigarette from her packet. 'Matthew's been a wonderful fillip, Lynny. But I've taken advantage of him. I'm afraid that's true.'

'Advantage?'

'Well, everyone knows he's got this "thing" about me – has had from the start. You should see the nudging and winking that goes on at The Bell.'

'Exactly what sort of *thing*?'

'A crush, I suppose. You know – the allure of the older woman!'

'You always denied it when the students used to tease you.'

'I didn't want them making a fool of him. I'm extremely fond of him. Heavens! If I'd been twenty years younger, I'd've been like Beth. I make no bones about that.'

'So, what happened last night?'

'He indulged me – he always does – letting me ramble on for hours, buying me drinks.'

'I wonder why.'

'That's it, you see. He can't tear himself away. It's all madly flattering at the time, but, afterwards, I feel horribly guilty. For his own sake, I ought to send him packing.'

'Well, *do*, then.' Lyn turned her toast under the grill. 'You're sure you're right about this "thing"? Has he actually admitted to it?'

'He doesn't need to.' Clare smiled to herself. 'You're still very innocent in some ways, Lynny. It's rather sweet.'

He stopped in the corridor and beckoned to her. Right in front of everyone, he called her name.

'Lyn,' someone said, 'you deaf or something? Beech is bellowing his head off!'

'What now?' Beth groaned. 'Another star role?'

Lyn broke away and the group shambled on towards the canteen, poring over a magazine, deploring this week's Top Ten. An obvious fix. You couldn't trust anyone.

'I love you, Lynny. That's not a lie.'

'Kissing her in the street! What's she supposed to think?'

'We're just friends. She knows that.'

'She thinks you're bats on her. So do all her friends. Why *do* you hang round her all the time?'

'I like her. She introduced me to that crowd at The Bell. I like them, too . . . Anyway, she talks a lot about you. And how else could I see you as much as I do. I wouldn't be able to turn up at your house any more.'

They stared at each other helplessly across the essential three-foot gap between them. 'People must be looking,' she whispered. 'Let's meet tonight.'

She told Clare she was going to Beth's. The lie slipped out easily. She didn't care. Consciences were a big bore. And they didn't stop you doing what you wanted to do, anyway – they just prevented you enjoying it properly.

They drove five miles to a market town called Moorbridge, and took the well-trodden path beside the wide river there.

Tarpaulined motor-launches and dinghies lapped against the bank. Lights shone from isolated portholes, stippling the water, and, overhead, strings of coloured bulbs, left over from Christmas, bobbed among the bare branches. They walked, hand in hand, now and then ousted from the track by jostling youths heading for the riverside pub half a mile further on. He drew her aside into a copse.

It was dark suddenly, and very still. He lined a hollow between thick tree-roots with his jacket, and they nestled there. 'We'll be found in the morning, dead of exposure!' she said.

He folded her into himself. 'I'll find us a place. Soon. Not the back seat of a car or a hole in the ground.'

'Will we make love?'

'We do already – every glance, every touch.'

'You know what I mean.'

He didn't answer. In their hollow, they moved and breathed as one. 'You know, I think if we were actually going all the way, we'd feel more separate,' she whispered. 'We'd have separate roles. As it is, we're both the same, aren't we?'

They lay in each other's arms for half an hour, only realizing when they drew apart, and stood up, how tightly the cold had gripped them. They chafed their numb arms and legs in alarm and stumbled stiffly back to the car. 'I'll find us a place,' Matthew breathed, wiping the tears from her eyes, 'where we don't have to wrench ourselves away from one another and step out into the middle of winter. And whatever love we make, we'll never be "separate". I can promise you that.'

'Was that a silly thing to say? Are you laughing at me?'

He snatched her up, clean off her feet, and whirled her round. 'My God, Lynny Mellor! You fill me with laughter!'

Two days later, Beth was cowering by the coat pegs. 'Something awful's happened!' She told her tale, mouth and voice quivering. She had been sending Matthew more notes – she knew it was daft; that was why she hadn't told Lyn earlier – and he'd handed the whole lot over to Miss Campion, the Year Counsellor. 'Rachel Pearson's sent hundreds, and he hasn't handed hers over. She writes them on foul, scented paper and he just thanks her for them. I'm going to tell Campion how he looks at me all the time.'

'Why on earth did you write?'

'I wanted to meet him again. I said I was going mad. I am, aren't I? And now he won't see me at all, apart from lessons, I suppose. And I've got to go and see Campion instead.'

The appointment was after school. Lyn leant against the wall by the main gate. Beth was a victim, like Clare. They ought to be told. They ought to have been told long ago . . . A car drew up beside her and Matthew wound down his window.

'I'm waiting for Beth. Did you have to do it?'

He nodded.

'Why didn't you tell me?'

'I don't want to talk about other people when I'm with you. Time's too short as it is.'

'It seems so unfair. Beth loves you, and you don't love her back, and half the world thinks she's off her head. And I love you, and you do love me back, and I've never been so happy in my life.' She bent down. Through the nine inch gap their faces and mouths met. Then the car was racing away down the road and Lyn was standing there, alive from head to foot!

The Hastingses sent for her – secretly. On no account was Beth to be told. 'How intriguing,' said Clare. 'What's it all about?'

'Matthew, I suppose. I told you, ages ago, that Beth was getting herself in a mess. You said you couldn't talk to him about his teenage girls, remember? You said that wasn't what he came to you for.'

It was a long time since she had been there, she realized, as she passed the Hastingses' front flower-bed, brimming with clusters of purple crocuses. Must have been before Christmas – the night of the party – the night of the first kiss . . . The door opened. Mr Hastings was agitated, beginning to help her off with her coat before she had undone the buttons. 'Beth's at the dentist. We haven't a lot of time.'

Mrs Hastings didn't get up. 'We're at our wits' end.' She looked weary, her hair dry, her face grey without its usual coats of paint. 'What's Beth up to? You must know. You've been her friend for years.'

'I didn't know she was up to anything.'

'Look, Lyn,' said Mr Hastings, 'no time for games. Is she on drugs?'

'Oh no,' said Lyn. 'I'm sure she's not.'

'Glue-sniffing?'

'No.'

'You don't have so much time for her now, though, do you? So you can't be absolutely certain. Is she in with another set? Do you actually know, nowadays, what she's up to?'

'I think so,' said Lyn. Her voice was wobbly all of a sudden. 'You make me feel it's my fault, Mr Hastings. I haven't meant to abandon her. There's so much exam work this year.'

'What you're saying is, she *might* be on drugs. You aren't sure.'

'I am sure. It's nothing like that. She's just . . . '

'Just what?' Both pairs of tormented eyes homed in on her.

'She's got herself into trouble with Mr Beech. You know . . . the English teacher. She's been writing him letters, and he's given them to Miss Campion. She's had to go for counselling.'

'Why weren't we informed? Why weren't we sent for?'

'She was desperate for you not to know.' Through the window, they all spotted Beth, turning in at the gate and

75

wheeling her bicycle past the window. She looked in. 'I shouldn't have told you,' said Lyn. 'I wish I hadn't. Parents don't have to know everything.'

Sometimes, when he came home unexpectedly from the pub with Clare, or when she glimpsed him at Cardy's, or even in a corridor at school, she found herself breaking into a quick sweat of panic. What if, without thinking, she just kissed him or said something spontaneous that gave the whole game away? Within minutes, there would be uproar, and everything would be over. Even in his absence, something might slip out accidentally. The more she loved him, the more he became part of her, and the more of herself she had to hide. One night, she dreamt she was struck dumb. It was the only way to be safe.

In lessons, she felt more secure, and when she had actually schemed a meeting. These were situations she could control. It was the chance enounters that were dangerous – when her joy might break through, of its own accord, and betray them both!

'God! I'm becoming such a fraud, I hardly dare breathe!' she told him, in the car, one night. 'I have to vet everything I say before I say it. I could easily come out with something you've told me, or mention being somewhere when I'm supposed to have been somewhere else!'

He nodded. 'That's how I feel when I'm with Clare. I *have* to see her, you know. I'm fatally drawn to her – like a criminal to the scene of the crime. Sometimes I think my mouth is going to open, all by itself, and start spilling out a confession. I find myself watching *her* mouth. I imagine the stream of invective . . . I like her. I really do. That makes it worse.' He leaned over the steering-wheel and stared out into the dusk. They were parked on a roughly turfed verge under a weeping willow. A frond or two trailed across the windscreen. He traced them with his forefinger, on the

76

inside of the glass. 'The trouble is, Lynny, my guilt doesn't stop at other people. . . . It reaches you, too.'

'*No*. I don't want it to. It doesn't need to.'

'What am I doing to you, Lynny? So young . . . '

She pulled him towards her. There was a feeling like flapping wings inside her chest. '*Shh*! You make us sound like other people. What's age got to do with it? We're just *us*.'

CHAPTER TWELVE

He started looking at her in class again – blatantly, she thought. As if he was past caring. People were so blind. They didn't notice. They put their hands up to ask questions and answer them; they groaned at excessive homework, and objected to low grades. Privately, they said he was the best teacher in the school. They wondered about his sex-life and decided he had sacrificed it to marking their books and preparing their lessons! Over the tops of their heads, Lyn blew him a kiss. They were so blind!

'Mrs Ryder says you're an exemplary class,' he said one morning. 'She wishes you were hers!' He was standing at the front, handing back exercise books. Spring sunshine was blazing in over the desks nearest the windows and he had rolled up the sleeves of his shirt. *Those arms have been round me*! It struck Lyn as funny that she'd never actually seen them before. Pupils stepped forward as he called out their names. 'Lyn Mellor!' *I love you*. As she flicked open her book to see her mark, a buff envelope slipped out and dropped to the floor. 'What's that?' whispered a neighbour. Matthew glanced at her sharply as she picked it up and tucked it away. It was break before she could lock herself in one of the girls' lavatories and rip it open. She stood in the smelly little cubicle and beamed. He had found a place. In the Easter holidays, they could have sole use of a private flat for ten days!

*

'Hey! You!' Simon walked on a few paces and jerked his head.

Lyn looked at him in surprise. Beside her, Beth heaved a caustic sigh. 'You'd better go and see what he wants. Obviously not me.' She walked on.

Simon pulled a face. 'What ails The Death?'

'She's not too keen on me these days. I told her parents something she didn't want them to know.'

'Ah, it's true then – all we hear about grand passion in the bike-sheds!'

'It's not funny. What d'you want anyway?'

He looked at her askance. 'An explanation, actually. How come, when I phoned you up last night, I got dear Clare rhapsodizing about how pleased she is we've got it together again?'

'Oh!'

'So?'

'I'm sorry, Simon.'

'I'm the alibi, aren't I? When you're seeing him, you say you're seeing me.'

'Not always.'

'What's so bad about him? Why's he the big, black secret?'

'Nothing's bad.'

'Married?'

She shook her head. 'Don't ask.'

'You're using me,' he hissed suddenly. 'Why shouldn't I ask? I don't bloody like it. He's a shit, driving you to this.'

Simon phoned her again that night, to invite her to a party to celebrate the publication of the school magazine. It was to be at Mr Beech's the evening after school broke up. 'I asked him if I could bring you. I said you'd given me a hand.'

'What did he say?'

'Seemed to think it'd be OK.'

'I'm awfully sorry, Simon, I've promised to go to the cinema with Beth. Her parents are taking her away after that. They want to get her mind off things.'

'*Him*, you mean!'

She had been preparing the ground for some days. She and one or two others from school were going to spend the holidays getting really fit, she'd told Clare – walking one day, cycling the next, swimming, tennis . . .

'Good Lord!' said Clare. 'I thought I'd have to endure you lolling round all day, mouthing beastly pop-songs! What's brought this on?'

'Your ignorant generation! You've half-killed us with junk food. All British teenagers are destined to heart disease and early graves. It's been on telly!'

She arrived downstairs, on the first day of the holidays, in her school track-suit, and gulped a cup of coffee in the kitchen. Outside, it was drizzling steadily. 'Sticking to the plan, regardless?' Clare was already at the table, in her dressing-gown, shuffling through some papers. 'We're having a Players' meeting here tonight. I hope to God Matthew turns up! I've shoved a reminder through Cardy's door. We want him to wangle Gledhill hall for us at Christmas.'

'What for?'

'*Puss in Boots*. I think I've just about talked everyone into it. Wouldn't Gran be tickled?'

'Oh, yes! She'd be barmy enough to approve.'

Clare stuck out her tongue and turned back to her papers. 'Be careful!'

Funny thing to say, Lyn thought, today of all days! Matthew had slipped an address into her hand, and she had tracked it down on a street-map – the other side of town. She pedalled slowly. Was it going to be all different? When she cycled back this way would *she* be all different? Did you really feel different once you'd done IT? People said you did, but half of them didn't know. You must still be *you* – just with another experience notched up. Like learning to swim, or flying for the first time. Of course, you had to take precautions. Matthew would handle all that side of it, presumably. You couldn't get to twenty-four and not have it all worked out. She stopped at a corner shop and bought a bar of chocolate. Maybe they wouldn't do it after all. They hadn't really talked about it much. But why else fix up the flat? Anyway, it had often been obvious he wanted to. So did she. It didn't really need saying. And they did love each other. They were always saying *that* . . . Anyone would feel nervous. Slightly. It was bound to feel peculiar, or hurt a bit, the first time. She was beginning to feel sick and threw most of the chocolate in a litter-bin. Better get there and get on with it! She jumped back on her bike and rode hard.

Sturrock Grove was on the south side – a newish block of flats set back from the main road behind fluttery beech hedges. Matthew's car was in the car park already. She chained her bike to a nearby post and made her way round to the front of the building, past oval flower beds bristling with dark shoots. Getting pregnant wasn't the only worry . . . There were all those diseases you could get . . . Maybe it had been better before, nipping off in the car for a quiet snog . . .

She was confronted by her own reflection in gleaming glass doors and combed out her damp hair before pushing through them, and setting off up the marble staircase opposite. As she turned the bend at the top of the flight, she was brought up short by the broad beam of someone down on her knees with a soapy cloth. 'Don't you worry! No one else does!' The cleaner paused as Lyn squeezed past, apologizing for stepping on the wet bit. She dropped her cloth in a bucket of suds and hauled herself to her feet. 'Who're you looking for?'

'Number five.'

'Mrs Ryder, that is. There's a young man in there for a week or two. Wanting him, are you?' She watched as Lyn reached the top of the stairs and set off uncertainly along a corridor. 'Blue door, straight ahead!' She carried on watching, only her red face and her shoulders visible. 'That's it. There's a bell at the side.'

The door opened as if on a spring. He looked boyish, Lyn thought, his hair ruffled as if he'd only just pulled his clothes on. 'That woman's all suspicious!' she whispered desperately. But, from his blank look, she guessed that no one was there any more – the cleaner had dropped to her knees again and was, presumably, once more lashing her cloth to and fro over the marble. 'She's out there washing the stairs. She said this was Mrs Ryder's place. She's bound to tell her.'

'It's Mrs Brass. When I see her again, I'll tell her I'm giving you some coaching! Come and have a cup of coffee. I'll talk to you about Sheridan and Spenser!'

The flat was small, with cream walls, and varnished floors, dotted with red rugs. Lyn perched self-consciously on a stool in the little kitchen. 'I don't feel normal. We don't seem like us at all.'

'Rubbish!' He spoke almost sharply, loading things on to a tray and leading the way into Win's sitting-room. 'Come here!' He sat on the sofa, arms outstretched. 'Give it a chance.'

'Where is Mrs Ryder?'

'South of France, I should think. She left yesterday.'

'She'd have a fit if she knew I was here.'

He nodded. 'She doesn't, though.' He pulled her down into the hollow of his shoulder. 'She never will.'

'Matthew . . . what's going to happen?'

'Happen?'

'What're we going to do here?'

'We're just going to be together. Uninterrupted. Relaxed. Not checking over our shoulders, like rabbits, all the time.' He swung his feet up and lay back, his head resting on cushions. 'Lie with me.'

'Isn't there a bedroom?'

'Two.'

'Aren't we going to use one of them?'

He leaned up on an elbow and gazed at her. 'I'm going to love you, Lynny,' he said slowly, 'but I'm not going to make love to you.'

'Oh! Very nicely put!' She pulled away abruptly. 'How come you're deciding everything? We're not at school now.'

'I'm not. At least, I wasn't meaning to. But it's only sensible to have one's mind made up about some things. Otherwise it's easy to make mistakes.'

'Like getting carried away, you mean – by mad spontaneous passion, or something?'

'Yes.' He turned away and started drinking his coffee. She could hear the sound of his measured gulps.

'Seems to me, it was a million times more fun groping round in your car.' His back view struck her as ridiculous suddenly – the jersey too tight, the tufts of hair sticking, bolt upright, out of the top of his head. 'Can't think why you've fixed us up here at all. That woman's never going to believe I've come trotting up to spend the day chastely chit-chatting about books. Like you and Mum, for God's sake! It's not normal.'

He jumped round suddenly, and gripped her tightly by the arms, pinning her down. 'Isn't it possible for us to be in bliss, just as we are, Lynny? You know I want you. I'm plagued to death by the guilt of it.'

He looked mad. Fleetingly, she was reminded of Beth. 'Shhh,' she whispered. 'Shhh. I'm sorry. I felt a fool, that's all. It wasn't what I thought . . . Not that I'd really thought anything – or not enough, anyway. You're probably right.'

'Am I?' He buried his face in her neck. She could feel his mouth moving against her skin as he spoke. 'When you're here, I feel "right". But not when you're not. Then I feel *wrong*, Lynny.'

'Shhh.' She could feel the wings beginning to flap again in her chest. 'I hate you talking like that. It makes me think you're working up to getting rid of me.'

At lunch-time, he cooked spaghetti for her, poking it in the boiling water and testing it with his fingers till they were red with the heat. She found a tin of meat sauce in one of Win's cupboards and they poured it over the top and sat at the kitchen table, eating, side by side, from one big plate. While he was washing up, she found Win's record collection and put on a Beatles L.P. He stood in the doorway, hands dripping, watching her dancing on her own. 'You're so beautiful, Lyn.'

She held out her arms and he joined her, moulding her into himself, kicking Win's rugs aside as they swayed round the room. When the record ended, they stood locked together for a long time, then he turned away heavily and leaned over the record-player.

'It's insane!' she screeched. 'You can't keep pushing me off.' The pitch of her voice surprised her. She saw him jump. Before he could move or speak, she had dashed into the hall, snatched her anorak from a peg, and fled. Outside, in the car-park, she waited in the rain. She expected him to come looking for her, but he didn't, and, after a while, she unlocked her bike and pedalled slowly away.

At dusk, she crept back. The marble stairs and steel banisters gleamed under humming neon lights. She stood outside Win Ryder's door, ringing her bell for five minutes, but no one came.

The next day, she stayed in bed till after eleven o'clock, a blanket pulled over her head. 'What's happened to the fitness campaign?' said Clare.

I'm still a virgin. Lyn took the cup of tea Clare was offering. *I can look my mother in the face. I'm not a total fraud.*

It was afternoon before she went back to Sturrock Grove. Mrs Brass wasn't there. No one saw her.

Matthew opened the door without a word and, straight away, drew her into a room she hadn't seen before. Weak sunlight was slanting through Venetian blinds over a wide double-bed. The bedspread was pulled back. Her mouth turned dry. 'What . . . ?' she croaked.

He was unbuttoning her blouse, his eyes holding hers. He still wasn't speaking. Had he changed his mind, then? Did he think they should be doing it after all? Did he think *she* still thought that? . . . *Did* she? . . . '*No!*' she gasped.

From then on, they were at peace. It was a wet week. She arrived every morning, dripping and chilled through. He had coffee waiting. They drank it together at Win's big front window, heads touching, watching the blossom trees below shivering like guests at a wet garden-party. 'Everyone outside looks so miserable,' she whispered. 'No one else in the world is in love!'

They perfected the art of cooking spaghetti and, on Matthew's birthday, Lyn donned an apron and concocted a chocolate cake, using a sticky old recipe book of Win's. She ran out, through the rain, for two packets of cake-candles and a frill. That day, she brought some of her own records from home and taught him Gledhill's own particular style of disco-dancing. It was one of the few times she ever heard him laugh aloud. They didn't go anywhere near Win's bedroom again, until the last day . . .

They had been subdued all morning. Over lunch, as she wound the last of the spaghetti round her fork and sucked it into her mouth, she whispered, 'How can we ever go back to being as we were?'

'I don't suppose we can.'

'Will you be able to find somewhere else?'

'I'll try.' He pushed his plate away, unfinished.

When she reached out and took his hand, it was to comfort him. It was to comfort him that she led him along to Win's room. It was dusty now, and very still. She closed the door behind them and began to step out of her clothes. She didn't look at him as she climbed into the bed. The sheets were ice-cold.

CHAPTER THIRTEEN

Beth came back from her holiday remarkably restored, at least as far as one could tell. There had been a guy at the guest-house – a bit younger than her, but not much. He had asked her out. Half-way through a boring old Western, he'd started kissing her. Properly. Later on, he'd done quite a bit more than that.

'You've got over all the heartbreak, then?' said Lyn. 'Just like that!'

Matthew had been gone a week. That last wet day, they had clung together in the big bed until it was time for her to go. Around them, the room had grown dark till, at last, she could only just see his head, like a black football, against the pillow. 'I'll have to go, Matthew.' She had switched on the lamp. 'Mum'll be wondering.' She had dressed quickly. 'Do you love me?'

He had nodded. But she had cycled away frighteningly convinced that he didn't – that he hadn't wanted any of what had just happened and that he would never love her again, because of it. From the main road, she had looked up at Win's front window and he had been outlined there, waving. A long way off. Waving . . .

'What've you been up to?' Beth was saying.

'Nothing.'

'You're not jealous, are you? You could go out with Simon Reid again, if you wanted to.'

'I do see him sometimes.'

She had seen him two days ago. She had phoned him up and asked him to come round. But as soon as he'd arrived, trying not to look hopeful, she had known it wasn't going to be any good.

'You're bored to tears,' said Clare. 'That's what's wrong with you. Why has the keep-fit campaign fizzled out?'

I've done it, Mum.

Clare was busy now. The Players had, indeed, decided on *Puss in Boots*, and she had volunteered to organize the whole thing, as well as take the part of Puss. 'I wish I'd got it going while Gran was still alive. She'd 've enjoyed it all so much.'

'Is Matthew going to be in it?' *That's who I did it with.*

'Heaven knows! He's away. I'm quite glad, actually. I've been able to get on with things. He's an awful distraction when he's here.'

Do you still love me, Mum?

'He's bound to be back for the start of term. I'll need to badger him about booking the school hall for us. He'll be amazed at how I've got on.'

Does he think about how I'm getting on? Does he wonder if I'm all right? We weren't going to do it – why did we? Now I can't think of anything else. Still, at least he took precautions. Condoms! That's how they go on! Thank God, anyway. 'Safe Sex.' Nothing to worry about. But I am worrying. All the time. I can't forget. It does make you different. It makes everything different. How do you go back to not doing it? . . . ?

Lyn remembered the days of 'not doing it'. So long ago! The 'innocent' days! There had been the time they had read *The House at Pooh Corner* together, using different voices for the animals. They had gone off in the car afterwards, in the one blink of sunshine there had been all week, and found a good stream for playing 'Pooh-sticks'. And, another time, she had run herself a bath at Win Ryder's, and been quietly steaming in it, with her eyes shut, when he had crept in and emptied a jug of cold water over her. She had shot up in the air, howling and splashing, and he had been standing there, grinning his head off.

'I heard from Matthew today,' Cardy sighed. 'Unwelcome news. I'm a bit down.'

'What's happened?'

'Problems with the sister. She misses him. She's making life impossible for Mrs Beech.'

'Can't she get help?'

'It seems not.'

'Well, what are they going to do?'

Cardy shrugged. 'Sounds to me as if he's decided to go back.' She plucked an envelope from the mantelpiece, pulled out a letter and scanned it, running a thin brown finger along the lines. 'Yes . . . Here we are . . . "If we can't fix something more satisfactory for Anna, it looks as if I should come home for a while. Don't worry, your advice hasn't fallen on deaf ears!" I warned him against letting the situation swallow him up, you see. He could waste his whole life, quite easily, running round after that girl. His mother knows that. "But Lamford's just a touch too distant. I ought to be near enough to come in and help in an emergency." ' Cardy folded the letter up carefully and pushed it back in its envelope. 'You see, Lynny? He's going to leave us. I suppose it's the right thing.'

'He'll be missed at school.' Lyn got clumsily to her feet.

'He'll be missed here,' said Cardy. 'But he's never been one to shirk responsibilities. I admire that in him.'

Lyn nodded dumbly. *He's shirking me*. Outside, she bolted blindly for home. Clare found her later, stone-still, under her bedclothes. She stroked her forehead. 'Poor Lynny. What's wrong?'

88

'You still look peaky, Lyn,' said Mr Hastings, reaching round a candlestick for the cheese-board. 'Flu, was it? – you remind me of our Beth when she was down with Beechitis. I take it there's none of that there 'ere!' He laughed loudly and patted her arm. 'There, there, m'dear. Just a joke.'

Two days and he'll be back. How long for? Doesn't he love me? Did he ever? Was that a joke?

CHAPTER FOURTEEN

He looked just the same – laden with books – as the very first time. He gave them out and sent someone for more. He came round the front of his desk and propped himself against it. She waited for his eyes . . . She felt clammy and short of breath . . . Why was he looking at Cicily Stowe all the time? Ugly lump! Why wasn't he searching her out? Perhaps he'd spotted her the moment he came through the door. Perhaps he didn't trust himself to look again. *Lovers*! She hadn't stopped thinking about it. Had he?

He looked, in the end. At least, she thought he did. Just for a second. Then his eyes slid fishily away. They turned and swam back, but she couldn't hold them. When the bell rang, he read out a list of people he needed to talk to, about their work. Lyn was one. She queued, last in line. He'd want that. 'Ah, Lyn!' He opened his case and searched among books as the classroom emptied. 'I've got something for you.'

'Matthew . . . '

'Read it first.' He handed her an envelope. 'Go somewhere quiet. Try to understand. Whatever else, *believe*.'

'Believe what?'

Outside in the corridor, a crisp clacking of heels came to a sudden halt, and Win Ryder looked in at them. 'I trust I'm not interrupting.'

'Just coming, Win.' He scooped his bag under his arm and went off along the passage with her. Lyn gazed at the envelope for a second, then ripped it open. 'Darling Lynny. It has to stop . . . '

When she came out of the classroom, she could see that Matthew and Mrs Ryder had come to a standstill only a few yards further on. They turned and looked at her. Afterwards, she kept on seeing them, slowly turning, fixing her with froggy eyes . . .

Beth was in seventh heaven. She had had a letter too – from the boy-friend. She flapped it in Lyn's face. 'I suppose I could let you see it. I suppose it's not *that* personal!'

'It doesn't matter.'

'Don't you want to? Look, he's sent a photograph. He looks better than that really.'

'Very nice.'

'Do you really think so, Lyn? You wouldn't touch him with a barge-pole yourself, would you? Go on, you can say. I won't mind.'

'I don't know,' said Lyn. She forced herself to look at Beth. Would it show – how she felt? Beth was so full of herself – would she notice?

'God!' said Beth. 'You look awful. What's wrong?'

'I don't know.'

'It's not me prattling on about Richard, is it? I'm not really that keen. I'm just trying to keep myself interested in anything male that isn't Matthew Beech!'

At night, she read and reread the letter. It was garbled. He had no right, with a brain like his, to write such gibberish. It didn't make sense. It made her cry. It made her shake with rage. In a way, he said, he felt proud of their love. It was something to shout from the roof-tops. 'But, oh, I feel the shame of it too – at times prostrated by it. Abject. To have introduced someone like you to the lies, the deceits, the dark corners . . . Despicable, Lynny. Am I despicable? I must go. (I must, in any case. My mother clearly still needs me. And, besides, Win Ryder knows something. I'm afraid Mrs Brass did tell her you were at the flat.) And you will be free again . . . Oh, I don't want this at all. I long for you. Most physically. Was it lust all along, then? Was that *all*? Was the only really honest moment that last night at Win's? We mustn't meet again. We're breaking too many truths and trusts. In the end, that breaks us . . . But I love you, Lynny. Whatever that means, it's all that is left to say.'

Crap! She screwed the letter up and tossed it in her waste-paper basket . . . She dived after it and straightened it out – tenderly. She pored over it . . . Between two and five in the morning, she scribbled different replies. How dare he walk out? What about *her* pride, and guilt, and love? He was wallowing and panicking – a gutless wimp. A '*runt*', as Nigel King had told her, months ago . . .

'Dear Matthew,' she wrote at last, 'I'll wait. The path of true love never . . . etc. This *is* true. And it *is* love. Your Lyn. P.S. I'm proud of the lust too. P.P.S. I'm dying to shout it from the roof-tops. It's other people's hypocrisy that stops us. That's their shame, not ours.'

She dozed after that and, at six, came to and sprang out of bed. Outside, the sun was risen but pale. Barnton Road was full of bird song and white blossom. She floated along it to the corner and turned left into Wellington Place. At Cardy's, she pushed her letter through the door and heard it plop firmly on the floor the other side. There. He would be all right now. It would *all* be all right. Poor Matthew!

'What in the world!' It was Clare, stock-still in the hall with staring eyes. 'Where have you been?'

'Nowhere. It's a fabulous morning.'

Clare blinked feebly. 'Communing with nature now, are we?'

'Sort of.'

'You look happy, anyway.'

Lyn nodded.

'That's good. Will it last?' Without waiting for an answer, Clare wandered back upstairs.

By breakfast, utter weariness had set in. The wave of elation had rolled on, leaving Lyn behind. She tried to eat.

'What's this about Matthew leaving?' said Clare, scraping the burn off a piece of toast. 'I haven't been able to sleep. Jean Scott told me. I felt a fool not knowing. I had to cover up by pretending I thought it was a secret. Cardy's known for ages, apparently. Didn't she tell you?'

'It's not true.'

'It is. He's already resigned, Jean says. A term's notice. I can't think why he hasn't said anything.'

It wasn't all all right. In lessons, he looked at her, but the looks were blank, not from deep inside himself any more. Not from anywhere. *I'm waiting. I know you'll come . . .*

'Is it the exams?' said Beth.

'Is what the exams?' Beth was a menace, prying and peering.

'You don't talk. You don't eat. Why don't you tell me what's wrong?'

'Nothing to tell.'

'Dad says your light's gone out.'

In English, she sat in the back row now, head down over her book, while his voice rumbled on, deep in its underground caverns. Once, she'd heard it in her ear, close, his breath whispering . . . rushing . . . roaring her name. Never again. The writing on her page blurred.

He stopped beside her in a corridor. 'Lyn?'

'Yes, Mr Beech.' Eyes down.

He murmured, 'You've got to do better than this, for both our sakes.'

'This is my best.'

He stopped her again, in the afternoon of the same day. 'Look at me, Lyn. I can't bear this.'

93

And three times the next week. 'Don't cut me off. Be kind. I love you.'

'Come back, then. What's stopping you? Not me.'

'What's going on with *him*?' said Beth, pinch-nosed. 'You're forever whispering in corridors.'

'I'm behind with essays.'

'He should be blasting you out, then, not jollying you along with little pep-talks.'

'You'll have heard various rumours, by now,' he said, in week three, standing at the front of the class. Her heart lurched. 'They're true, I'm afraid. I'm having to leave at the end of the term – for family reasons. I'm very disappointed. You've done some brilliant work for me. I had been looking forward to taking a lot of you through to A-level. All I can say is that Mrs Ryder will be carrying on where I leave off. She and I will liaise very closely beforehand. There won't be anything she doesn't know about your individual work, and your future plans, and your concerns generally . . . '

Will you liaise with Mrs Ryder about me, Mr Beech? And my individual concerns? Lyn's hand went up, but, before he could respond, she had stumbled to the door. In the cloakroom, she leaned against the tiled wall. She could see her white face in a small mirror opposite. Lyn Mellor – *betrayed*. She turned away from herself.

Sometime after that, she took to gazing at him again – straight, stony glances that were meant to kill. Let him suffer as she had. Let him feel the pain. One night, he came home from the pub with Clare.

'Matthew's managed to fix up the Gledhill hall for us,' said Clare, 'for *Puss in Boots*. It's such a shame he won't be here!'

'I could come back for it,' said Matthew. 'I don't want to disappear completely, you know.'

'You surprise me,' said Lyn. 'I thought that was exactly what you wanted to do.'

Clare was uncorking a bottle of wine. 'Take no notice of her, Matthew. She's been funny for weeks. She's never got over that fluey thing she had in the holidays. I'd adore you to keep in touch. You can stay here any time.'

'He's not serious, Mum.' Lyn gathered up her homework from the kitchen table and packed it into her bag. 'Once he's gone you'll never see hide nor hair of him again.' As she left, she turned. He was in pain all right. In her bedroom, she locked the door and wept into her hands – because she wasn't glad.

The Hastingses took Lyn away, at half-term, to a cottage they'd rented on the North Devon coast. Once or twice, Lyn had heard the tail-ends of conversations between Clare and Mrs Hastings. Everyone was worried about her. She couldn't care less. It was *their* fault, in the first place – theirs, and people like them. They couldn't be faced with naked truths, like schoolmasters falling in love with school-girls. Things had to be kept 'nice' for them. They mustn't be shocked. Sometimes, she imagined coming out with a bald announcement! At supper-time with Clare and the students, or over dinner at the Hastingses, swathed in her linen napkin, she rehearsed the words in her head. *Matthew Beech and I are lovers. We've done it, you know. The whole thing. Round at Win Ryder's.* But she didn't say a word – for his sake. He would hate her. He had come down on their side, hadn't he? Because of them, he had cut her off – wounding her far more than the truth would wound any of them.

The cottage was half a mile inland. Lyn and Beth shared a double bed with a badly stained horsehair mattress. 'I dread to think what's gone on on this!' sniggered Beth, covering it with a thick flannelette sheet.

Lyn gazed at her blankly. Last time she'd shared a bed, it had been with him.

'Are you OK? Did you want to revise all half-term? Are you wishing you'd stayed at home?'

'Course not. I've brought some books with me, anyway.' *He's gone up north again. Far away. Soon for ever.* 'There's nothing to stay at home for.'

Why wasn't he here? He, not Beth, should be wandering beside her down the twisting lanes, and lingering with her in the warm, windless hollows. On either side, the hedgerows grew high, and round, juicy spiders sat in their glinting webs. At noon, the wind dropped for an hour or two, and all was calm.

Down by the sea, despite the cloudless skies, it was breezy and cold. They wound up the legs of their jeans and squealed as the water raced towards them. Lyn heard herself and was astonished. She drew the air deeply into her lungs and, when Beth was out of earshot, closed her eyes and breathed his name into the rush of pebbles at her feet.

'You're going to be mad,' said Beth, on the way back for lunch one day. She had actually taken Lyn's arm and they were swinging along in step, faces upturned to the sun. 'I've been given strict instructions to find something out.'

'What?'

'Dad's idea. He thinks you might be pregnant.'

'He what!' Lyn snatched her arm away.

'I said you weren't.'

'Dead right! And who's the father supposed to be, or hasn't he worked that out yet?'

'He hasn't worked anything out. I knew you'd hit the roof.'

'Oh, I see! He calls me a slut and, if I react, that's "hitting the roof"!'

'He didn't call you anything. He just remembers me, that's all – how I got to the point where I'd have done just about anything for Matthew Beech.'

'That was you,' said Lyn. 'Not me.'

An hour later, in the middle of lunch, she rested her knife and fork against the side of her plate and leaned across to Mr Hastings. 'I am not, you'll be pleased to hear, in the family way. Nor has there ever been the ghost of a chance of it. I'm sorry you've been worried by such thoughts.'

Mr Hastings carried on eating, unperturbed. 'Finish your meal, lass,' he said, breaking off a large piece of bread and popping it in his mouth. 'No need to apologize.'

Clare was on her knees in the 'office'. She was wearing an old shirt and had tied her hair back with a pink silk stocking. 'Look, Lynny! I've just about cleared the lot. We can turn this into a cloakroom, like the Fishers. We can knock down that partition wall in between your bedroom and Gran's and buy a piano. It would make a perfect rehearsal room for The Players. We've got to have a new start. We can't hang on to the past.'

Lyn dumped her rucksack on the floor and leaned in the doorway, arms folded. The Hastingses had just dropped her off, and sped on home to open up the house and give it an airing while the sun was still shining. 'I'm not hanging on to anything.'

'Did you have a nice time?'

'Fine.'

'Not an overdose of Hastingses?'

'Not particularly.' Lyn appraised Clare coolly. 'Speaking of "hanging on" – isn't that what you're trying to do?'

Clare stood up and dusted herself down. 'What do you mean?'

'I bumped into Nigel outside. He dropped a few heavy hints about who's been coming round here while I've been away.'

'Players mainly. We're getting damn busy. Nigel's been in once or twice himself. He's Buttons, you know. Quite good actually . . . '

'I don't think he meant Players.'

Clare was becoming agitated. She was turning pink. 'If you mean Matthew, why don't you say so? Why all the mystery? He's only been back a couple of days. If he wants to come round here, I'm jolly pleased to see him.' She flounced past Lyn in the direction of the kitchen. 'I'm fairly fed up, as a matter of fact, at being made to feel guilty every time I let him over the doorstep. As if I'm tainting him or something. He's not going to come to any harm being friends with me, you know. I can think of loads of people more likely to lead him astray.'

CHAPTER FIFTEEN

Clare had planned a party to mark The Players' return to the boards. She had been talking about it for some time and, during Lyn's absence, had at last issued invitations – for Saturday, the day after her return from Devon. 'As far as you're concerned,' she'd told Matthew, 'it's to bid you farewell, and God speed, and come back as soon as you can.' In the note she'd dropped through the Hastingses' bolted-and-barred front door for Beth, she'd said it was by way of a little thank-you for looking after Lyn for the past week.

'It'll be a high note to end your half-term on,' she said to Lyn after lunch, watching her shaking the sand out of her shoes. 'I suppose you'll have to buckle down to exam slog afterwards. So try and enjoy yourself.'

'Beth will, anyway,' grunted Lyn. 'She likes goggling at your friends. She thinks they're all Laurence Olivier or someone.'

'I've invited Matthew – he's very popular with The Players. We're grateful to him for fixing up the hall.'

Lyn tucked the shoes, side by side, under her bed. 'No need to make excuses.'

Colin Winstanley arrived first, his damson face beaming round the front door. 'Not early, am I?' He patted Lyn on the bottom. 'You're turning out a real chip off the old block, Lynny!'

Later, when people had begun talking to one another, and filling up each other's glasses, Lyn slipped outside. It was a still night, heavy with cloud, though the rain had held off all day. The street was empty. As she turned back to the house, Nigel King emerged from next door, agleam in satin waistcoat and bow tie. 'Heavens alive, Mr King!'

'Tonight's the night!'

'Where's Joan?'

'Doesn't want to leave the kids.'

'I could keep popping round to check them for her. It'll be noisy later. She won't sleep.'

He shook his head. 'Best leave her to it. Very kind of you to offer.'

'I hope you're not going to drool over Mum all night.'

He was turning in at number forty-one. He caught her arm. In the dusk, she could see his top lip, twitching. 'I'm going to ignore that, Lynny. You're getting a damn sight too cocky these days.'

'I don't want you to ignore it. People make comments. It's not fair. Mum's not interested in you.'

'Oh, no? Who is she interested in, then?' He brought his face up close. 'As if we didn't know.'

The first raindrops spattered on their heads and they scuttled angrily up the steps. In the hall, Clare was receiving her guests, swaying graciously in a green, scoop-necked dress. Lyn wandered into the kitchen and propped herself against a radiator. She was wearing the white shift Clare had made her last Christmas, for the play. He had first loved her in that. He would come soon. He wouldn't be able to stay away . . .

Idly, she inspected the party-goers. Nearby, Ken Fisher was addressing an indifferent youth on the advantages of double-glazing. The youth was a total stranger – maybe a friend of one of the lodgers. He was running one of Clare's cocktail sticks along the insides of his finger-nails. When he'd finished, he flicked the stick in the air and wandered away. Ken's wife tittered to the room at large. 'At least it's not just me who finds him a bore!'

'I'm sorry,' said Lyn. 'He's not a friend of ours.' From where she was standing, she could see down the hall, between bobbing heads and shoulders, to the front door. It was opening, and half a dozen new arrivals were squeezing their way past immovable clumps of fellow-guests. At the back, a black head . . . Clare swung into view to remove dripping coats and jackets . . . 'See what the cat's brought in!' Nigel hissed in Lyn's ear.

Beth arrived, still glowing from the sea. '*He's* here!'

'You belong to another!'

'My knees are knocking.'

Lyn led her into the kitchen, where a mildly drunken throng of students was swarming round the table, tearing at the sticks of French bread, scattering huge crumbs over the floor. *He* was there already, talking to the Fishers. Lyn could feel his eyes. Burning. She reached for a bowl of crisps, stretching and twisting under the light dress. 'Could you two help me out?' said Clare. She thrust bottles of wine into their hands. 'I seem to be all shaky. Fill people's glasses up, will you? You'll enjoy it. It's a way of making sure you meet everyone.' She went over to Matthew and leaned against the wall, looking up at him. The Fishers withdrew. The word 'unseemly' lodged itself in Lyn's mind. Clare was unseemly – her laugh, her crazy, toppling hair, her plunging dress. She was bending towards Matthew now, a breast brushing against his upper arm.

'Is Clare absolutely plastered?' gasped Beth.

Lyn left her. She wove in and out of the shifting mass with her bottles. He would be watching her – the white, gliding form, dancing for him . . . For a second, her eye met his. She came close and filled his glass. Then she was off, circling out of reach. *Come with me.*

But he didn't.

The lights were off in the sitting-room, but a single candle burned on the mantelpiece and cigarettes glowed in the corners. A soulful record of Clare's was throbbing away on the turntable. 'Give us a dance, Lynny!' Colin Winstanley lumbered forward and grabbed her by the arm. A loop of dark wine shot from the top of one of her bottles. She felt it land, cold and wet, down the front of her dress. Across the room, she saw Beth surrendering to the arms of a stringy young man who had just joined The Players as a stage-hand. His mother had told Clare he was extending his social horizons. Beth was closing her eyes and leaning her cheek against the buttons of his open-necked shirt.

Lyn came out and stood in the hall, nursing her bottles against her front. The wine-stain had spread in a wide brown streak. She could feel lank strands of hair sticking to her brow. She was ugly now. He mustn't see her. No more dancing. Maybe he hadn't been watching her anyway. Probably unable to see past Clare and her eyes and her pleading bosoms. To her horror, she felt tears welling up right here in front of everyone. She dumped her bottles on the floor beside the wall, and shot to the front door. Outside, she turned her face up into the rain, and started to cry.

A quick shaft of light fell across the steps as someone opened the front door and darted out. He was there, swallowed up in shadows as he closed the door behind him. Then he was leaping down towards her. 'Lynny! You're getting soaked!'

'I don't care.'

'You're a sea-gull! Black-headed! Wet from the sea!'

'You're pissed!'

'Did you want me to follow you? I couldn't stop myself.'

'I've been wanting you to for weeks.'

He hugged her, letting out deep sighs as the rain pelted down, dripping from their hair to their eyes, soaking through their clothes to the warm skin . . . 'I've got the car, Lynny. Come on.'

'You're not fit to drive.'

'I won't, then. Come on.'

It was parked under a street-lamp, twenty yards away. They jumped in and clung together, as the rain drummed on the roof and streamed down the windows. 'It's like the very first time,' she whispered. 'I thought you were going to kiss me then, but you didn't.'

'A fool, Lynny! Such a fool!'

Nigel scurried back towards the house, then stopped. He turned round, and sneaked back to the car again – softly! softly! Oh, yes! It was them, all right! The slight, white form of the one, and the other with those puny, artistic shoulders . . .

Back in the sitting-room, there was a lull. Nigel stood in the doorway, collecting himself. Clare had turned on a light and was attempting to open a window. She wasn't going to be responsible for mass suffocation, she said. People were standing a little apart from their partners of the last half hour or so, regarding them shiftily, wondering whether to move on. Beth was obviously regretting her part in extending the stringy stage-hand's horizons; she was looking round, rather frantically, for Lyn . . .

'Clare!' Nigel threw his voice forward, not an actor for nothing. 'Clare, you probably ought to know what's going on outside . . .'

CHAPTER SIXTEEN

The next fifteen minutes or so, Lyn never forgot – from the impact of the first fist on the car roof, to the debagging of Matthew Beech, in the middle of Barnton Road, by a mob of howling students. All the time, the rain beat down. Up and down the street, curtains parted. 'Go back, Lyn!' Matthew roared. 'Go on!' She left him, half-drowned, half-naked, under the neon light. The students tossed his trousers at his feet and ran off too.

On the doorstep of number forty-three, Joan King was standing with an owl-eyed infant perched on her arm. 'In the name of God . . !' was all she said.

Inside, a remarkable sobriety had overtaken everyone. People held their breath as Lyn came in. 'Are you all right?' said Clare. She was chalk-white. As Lyn nodded, she wheeled on the rest of them. 'Boggle! Boggle! Had your money's worth?' She fixed Nigel with a glittering eye. 'The party's over!'

Seconds later, there were only the two of them left – plus Beth, waiting for a taxi. 'It's all Nigel King's fault,' she quavered. 'It's terrible, what he said.'

'What did he say?'

'Oh, you know – about you and Matthew.'

'I shall never forget what he said.' Clare stared ahead, still ashen, the circles round her eyes and lips alarmingly blue. 'Each word is imprinted on my mind. He said: "That wimp of a teacher you think so much of is

104

obviously intent on deflowering your daughter, under your very nose."'

'There's nothing to deflower,' said Lyn. 'That happened a long time ago. Matthew and I have been in love for months.'

The doorbell rang. After several seconds, a mouth applied itself to the letter-box and let rip a piercing whistle. *'Taxi!'*

As Beth picked up her coat, Lyn shrank away to her bedroom and locked the door. People had obviously been using her bed for private purposes. She stared in dismay at the rumpled blankets. Maybe this pair had been in love too – but, somehow, that wasn't how it looked. Apparently, it wasn't how she and Matthew looked either, to Clare and Beth.

'Can I come in?' It was Clare, tapping lightly.
'Tomorrow.'
'Let me in.'
'Go to bed, Mum.'
'Was it true, what you said?'
'Yes.'

Next day, the visitations started early. Cardy came first – at eight o'clock. Lyn opened the door. 'Mum's still in bed.'

'You'd better get her up, then. Matthew's gone. Disappeared into the night, like a criminal!'

'He'll be back.'

'He's taken everything. He won't be back.' Cardy strode down the passage to the kitchen and sat herself at the table, eyeing the edible remains of the party with disgust. 'I'll have a cup of coffee, Lynny, if you don't mind. I'm staying till I know . . . '

After that, there was Rachel Bishop's mother, standing, four-square, on the doorstep, ready to back any official complaint Clare cared to make. Rachel had been doolally ever since that young man arrived; she'd be quite honest

105

about it. How come the staff had turned a blind eye to what was going on? It was time the governors were informed . . .

Finally, Mrs Hastings arrived, tapping shakily at the front door. She perched on the pouffe, sipping a cup of tea and wishing desperately that Mr Hastings had come in with her, instead of waiting outside in the car. 'I just wanted to say it could so easily have been Beth,' she whispered. 'You mustn't think it was Lyn's fault, that's all. He obviously had a way with them. I'm sure if Beth had had the chance . . . It's an awful thing to say . . . I just mean, don't be too hard on her, that's all.'

'I wouldn't dream of it,' said Clare.

She and Lyn didn't start clearing up till the afternoon. Clare stood in the middle of the kitchen, knocking out ashtrays against the side of a metal bin. 'Well?'

'Well, what?'

' "In love", you said.'

'We haven't been seeing each other this term, though. He felt guilty.'

'Guilty?'

'With being on the staff.'

Clare carried the ashtrays over to the sink and began running them under a gushing tap. 'And he . . . you know . . . you made love, did you?'

'Sort of.'

'Oh?'

'Just the once.'

'Ah.'

'I don't suppose it counts, really. He went away afterwards and, when he came back, he refused to see me again. Till last night.'

Clare sat down and leaned her elbows on the table. Drips from her wet hands ran down her forearms. 'He gave every impression of adoring me, didn't he?' she said carefully. 'I've spent the night thinking it through, from the beginning. "Besotted", people said.'

106

'He did like you. He said so lots of times.'

'In love with the mother in me. I said that months ago. I wasn't joking. I was glad he could see that side of me.'

'He's got his own mother.'

'He's had to be man of that house, though, from the age of six. That's when his father died.'

'Well, he's good at taking charge and looking after people. He looked after me.'

'Did he? You've been miserable for weeks. I hoped I was looking after you.'

'Before that.'

Clare glanced up. 'I looked after him too, Lynny.'

'I know.'

'In ways you don't know.' Clare clasped her hands firmly on the table and stared at them. 'It was right at the beginning. He was lonely. I was just picking myself up after Gran. I'm afraid we rather fell into each other's arms . . .'

She looked up as there was a rush of feet towards the door. Lyn was standing there, shaking. She let out a thin screech. '*Don't*! Don't you say another word!'

'I've been thinking about it all night. I'm sure he did fall in love with you, Lynny. He certainly seemed to fade away from me. I tried not to mind. I thought he was just growing up. I suppose he was. I think he did love you, Lynny.'

Lyn's voice was a strangled hiss. 'Well, shut up, then, you *slag*! What are you trying to do? Kill it? Make sure I vomit at the thought of him? Why don't you keep your stinking secrets to yourself?' She turned and tore down the hall and out of the house.

'Oh – for a second, I thought it might be him,' sighed Cardy. It was early evening and she'd been dozing in the kitchen. 'I didn't get a wink last night. I don't know why he's gone, you know. Clare wouldn't say. Are you going to tell me? Is that why you've come?'

107

'Not really,' muttered Lyn. It seemed that Cardy wasn't going to let her in. They stood, regarding each other blankly across the threshold. 'I don't know, either.'

'Of course you do!' Cardy grunted. She opened the door wider and stumped off to the kitchen, leaving Lyn to follow.

It was an old woman's house again already. Cardy had obviously spent the day scouring and putting things to rights – no jacket slung over the knob at the foot of the stairs, no newspaper discarded on the hall-table, or pile of freshly-ironed shirts waiting to be carried upstairs.

'Can I stay here, tonight?' Lyn said. 'Like I used to. Now he's gone, can I have my bed back again?'

Not that he has gone! Not really. He's pretending. We're all pretending. At Cardy's, it was easy to see that the thing was a hoax. Nobody could disappear like that! He'd be back. There'd be questions to answer, but . . . *What questions? Not now . . .*

All evening, she and Cardy reminisced feverishly about times long before Matthew had ever been heard of. They made each other laugh aloud. Lyn heard herself at it and marvelled. Maybe she was mad.

At bedtime, she plodded slowly upstairs. Cardy was phoning Clare. 'You should do it yourself, Lynny,' she'd protested. 'She won't want to hear from me, you know. I said my piece this morning!' Outside the bedroom door, Lyn paused, heart thumping. *I'll go in and he'll be there! He'll have sneaked his way in without us hearing. We'll sleep together in the old truckle bed and Cardy will never know!*

The room was empty, the bed already made for her, the bare shelves and mantelpiece and chest of drawers polished to a high sheen. Lyn stood in front of the mirror. Only hours ago, had it been full of him, as he hurled his belongings into boxes and bags? Had he come up close, at the last minute, and peered into it, bidding himself farewell in this place? Had he known who he was? Had he thought anyone else knew – would ever know . . . ?

108

At two o'clock in the morning, long after she heard the snap of Cardy's light going out, Lyn got into bed herself. She had been dreading it – climbing into his coffin. She pulled the bedclothes up around her – his shroud. She shivered. He had never been closer . . . He had never been further away . . .

She didn't sleep. In her head, she could hear his voice again, as once she used to hear Gran's – those last words, over and over. She tossed and turned, drowning everything out. She buried her head in his pillow.

At school, first thing in the morning, people either obviously didn't know a thing, or else obviously did. But, by break, those in the latter category far outnumbered those in the former. Lyn looked in vain for someone to chat to about nothing in particular. Everyone wanted to know more – from the horse's mouth. Everywhere, smirking faces waited for her to tell.

Beth was absent. 'Could hardly blame her in the circs!' someone said.

'What was it like, Lyn?'

'Was he any good?'

'What've you got that the rest of us haven't?'

A yob called George Halliwell started heavy breathing. 'Was he kinky, Lyn? What did you have to do for an A?'

But the Eng Lit people found nothing to joke about. Lyn arrived two minutes before the class was due to start, and was met by total silence. In the back row, Sarah Tucker was sobbing into a handkerchief. 'It's not a tragedy,' said Mrs Ryder kindly. 'It seems like one today but – honestly – it isn't. Of course you're going to miss Mr Beech. We all are. But at least, as far as the work goes, I can take you through the exact revision course that you would have done with him. Next month, you'll all sail through those papers – standing on your heads if need be!'

'You've wrecked it for all of us,' someone hissed into Lyn's ear as she gathered up her books at the end. 'The most important exams of our lives, and you manage to cheat us out of the best teacher.' It was a girl called Rose MacInnes, tall and willowy, with alabaster skin. Bright spots were burning in each cheek. The other members of the class crowded behind her. 'Samantha said she saw you blowing him a kiss, once. None of us believed her but she was right, wasn't she? You've been chucking yourself at him all year. It's entirely your fault he's gone. He didn't like you specially, you know. Any of us could have had him. We didn't force ourselves . . . '

After school, Lyn slunk for cover down the passageway that led to Baby Quad. On the pavement outside, people would be waiting to waylay her with their gibes and nosiness. She sank down near the spot where she'd seen him talking to Beth . . . ages ago . . . before Christmas . . . before any of it, really. She dropped her head in her hands and didn't look up when footsteps approached.

'Only me.' Simon squatted beside her.

'I suppose you've heard.'

'Various versions.'

'What d'you think?'

'I've had my suspicions for ages.'

'He's gone. It's all unreal. I've got to see Campion tomorrow.'

In the end, she let him walk with her as far as Barnton Road. He carried her bag, swinging it from his lanky shoulder, having the sense not to speak. 'I think I'd rather go the last bit on my own,' she said. 'I did a bunk last night. I want to think about what I'm going to say to Mum.' He handed over her bag. He probably wanted her to be grateful but she didn't feel anything except relief at the sight of him departing. She wanted Clare. She wished she hadn't run out on her last night. They were best together – like after Gran died. She hadn't done a bunk then.

110

'Ah!' Clare was at the kitchen mirror, smoothing cream into the lines round her eyes. 'You're back!'

'School's been awful. They're all at me.'

'Beth?'

'She wasn't there.'

'Give it a week. Nine days' wonder. You'll see. How are you, apart from that?'

'OK.'

'He wasn't the sort who liked mucking people up, Lynny. He mucked himself up most of all, if you think about it.'

'I'm trying not to think about it.'

Clare began to dab powder carefully over the cream. 'I'm popping out, Lynny. Won't be long. I've decided to back down, you know. They need a young thing for "Puss". They'll have to face up to it.'

Lyn nodded slowly. 'Mum . . . you and Matthew . . . I never really thought of you like that . . . with anyone . . . '

Clare closed her compact with a snap and popped it into her battered shoulder bag. She took out a lipstick, tried it first on the back of her hand, then leaned busily into the mirror again. 'I know what you mean,' she mumbled. 'I hadn't exactly thought of you, either . . . '

After she had gone, Lyn leaned her head on the table and closed her eyes. Behind her, a fly buzzed and bumped against the window. She got up and let it out. Then all was still. The sun beat in on her back, its heat spreading . . . 'Lynny!' – his voice again. 'Forgive me.' Oh, he *had* loved her! He had clung to her! 'Lynny!' – through the pounding of the rain – ' . . . *Let me go*!'

CHAPTER SEVENTEEN

It was a hot, heavy summer. At school, once exams were over, people lazed around the tennis courts, swinging their rackets idly through the air, waiting for their turn. One or two enterprising teachers took lessons out of doors, under the one tree of any size in the grounds. It was a sycamore. Lyn fanned herself with its long-stemmed leaves and thought of Matthew, while others gradually forgot him. At home, she wrote him long letters and tore them up.

'*Let me go!*'

She wept, often at night, but never as overwhelmingly as that first afternoon. Clare had returned to find her sobbing convulsively. She had held her for a long time.

During the holidays, they set about redecorating the whole of the ground floor. Builders came in and pulled down the partition wall, making one big room again. 'We'll have cultured little soirées in here!' said Clare. She moved Gran's armchair through from the sitting-room. 'I shall sit in this,' she said, 'and grow old gracefully.'

Lyn was sleeping upstairs again, in her old bedroom. From its window, at the front of the house, you could see right over to Wellington Place, the backs of the little terraced houses. She and Matthew could have waved to each other if they'd thought . . . Sometimes, at dusk, she pretended she could see him there, in the shadows.

In the middle of August, Simon Reid left her as well. She probably couldn't give a damn, he said, looking down at the toes of the white trainers he'd bought for the summer, but he felt he should tell her, in any case, that she couldn't count on him any more. Not in the old way. He'd still be around, of course. He hoped they'd be friends.

Lyn agreed. Actually, she thought, she was all right for friends. There was Beth. Bit by bit, at last, she had told her everything. 'I'm really glad,' Beth had whispered, '*really* glad you've told me. It's half-killed me but I'm going to survive.'

'It's more than half-killed me,' said Lyn.

'You're going to survive too. And we *are* friends now. We weren't before.'

One baking, shadowless midday, Lyn was stumbling down Barnton Road with two half-gallon tins of paint. Every so often, she stopped, dumped them heavily on the pavement, and stood, flexing her arms, before the next haul. On either side, the fronts of the houses were flaking and crumbling in the sun, as they had, every summer, for a hundred years. She approached forty-one, dully aware of a car crawling along behind her. She didn't turn. As it slipped past, she stopped dead and shaded her eyes, heart pounding. *The Mini*! It hovered a few yards ahead, shimmering like a huge bubble. *Him! . . . It can't be*! Light dazzled her. He was stopping. She would run . . . jump in . . . roar away with him . . .

For a moment, the car seemed to wait: it filled the street . . . Lyn didn't move. Then, with a whoosh, it leapt forward, raced towards the main road and vanished.

She stood, just where she was, eyes closed. *Had* it been him? Could she have made him stay? Had he wanted her to?

At last, she opened her eyes. She bent down and slowly

picked up the tins of paint. Actually, it didn't matter who it had been. For that second, she had *believed* it was him . . . And she had just stood there . . . letting him go . . . knowing he would never be back. She had made that choice. She *had*.